CW01212527

Double Life Insurance

Bob Able

Bob Able Books

**This new book was presented
by Bob Able, the author.**

Please give it back to a charity shop when you have read it
so that it can be sold again to make more money
for worthwhile causes!

Copyright © 2022 Bob Able

All rights reserved

The characters and events portrayed in this book are fictitious. Any similarity to real persons, living or dead, is coincidental and not intended by the author.

No part of this book may be reproduced, or stored in a retrieval system, or transmitted in any form or by any means, electronic, mechanical, photocopying, recording, or otherwise, without express written permission of the publisher.

Double Life Insurance

Dedicated to Bee, for putting up with me.

A Bob Able Book

www.amazon.com/author/bobable

email: bobable693@gmail.com

Chapter 1

Martin Dartnell-Parkes had been with Stiffhams Estate Agents, Surveyors and Auctioneers for nine weeks, and been paid twice already.

It was only the basic salary at this stage, but when the sales started coming through, Mr Brownlow, the Branch Manager, had said they would see about putting him on commission. Even so, having an actual salary was a terrific novelty for Martin who, having just left school, had never had such riches in his life.

His mother had got him the job of course, through her contacts at the golf club, but Martin had managed to hush that up, so far at least, and he had begun impressing his growing circle of friends with his generosity at the local bar.

He was excited for the future and today his training took another step forward when Mr Brownlow took him to measure up a house for the first time, to put it on the market.

Martin knew the owner of the house in question slightly. She helped out at the school library sometimes and would probably remember him, he thought.

Sylvia Pendle was something of a mysterious woman to Martin and his school friends. She was tall and bony, with wild hair of an indeterminate colour and pale grey penetrating eyes that seemed to be staring straight through you. She habitually wore billowing translucent dresses which always seemed to be pale grey.

Miss Pendle, as Martin knew her, was some sort of artist, or was she a writer? He couldn't be sure. When she helped out in the school library, she gave a literary appreciation class thing for sixth formers who were interested, alongside Mr Jenkins, the Head of English.

Not being compulsory, Martin never bothered with those of course, so he had no first-hand knowledge of what she did there.

He did know she was recently divorced and now wanted to sell her house to move to some kind of commune in Wales. Martin thought it was all rather hippy.

Mr Brownlow parked his smart BMW just around the corner from Miss Pendle's house, explaining that it didn't do to be ostentatious with clients who were in what he called "straightened circumstances".

Martin had only a vague grasp of what that meant and no experience of life for people who did not fit into his parents' comfortable style of living. He knew there were poor people, of course, but he didn't think he had ever met one.

He wondered if Sylvia Pendle got paid to work at the school library, now that she was clearly beyond retirement age, and if she had to live on what she earned there.

The house they had come to see was an end of terrace. Quite modern, and rendered on the outside in a sort of pale grey colour which, Martin thought, was very similar to the floaty dresses Miss Pendle wore. The grey was relieved by a very bright green door framed by wind chimes and a fluffy 'dream catcher' thing which flopped about in the wind.

When Miss Pendle opened the door, she seemed even thinner than he remembered and was wearing her usual opaque pale grey wrap-around dress.

When her eye came to rest on Martin he realised, to his horror, that he had been staring at her breasts which, with the light coming from behind her, were quite visible through the material.

Martin blushed to the roots of his gingery hair and stammered out a 'Good morning', before dropping the pen he had been told to hold and almost losing his grip on the blue plastic clipboard which was part of the essential paraphernalia of his new trade.

Now invited into the lounge, Martin and Mr Brownlow looked around.

Martin was vaguely aware that there was virtually

no furniture in the room, just a low wide chair with thin, uncomfortable-looking, grey foam cushions, a glass coffee table, several bookcases, and some bits of bamboo in a big flowerpot beside the arch that led to the dining area. What he could not fail to notice, however, was the enormous impressionistic painting on one wall; and what it depicted shook Martin to the core.

It was a stylised view of a big white sofa with a long, stick-thin female form stretched out on it. This female was quite naked and as Martin's gaze reached the head end of the picture he caught sight of the penetrating pale grey eyes and realised, to his horror, that the artist's model was none other than Miss Sylvia Pendle, one time library assistant at his old school!

Mr Brownlow was prattling on about the state of the market and seemed quite unperturbed by the giant overbearing artwork, but Miss Pendle looked at Martin just as he looked away from it, and a slight knowing smile crossed her face.

Martin shuddered and hoped she hadn't noticed.

Before they arrived, Mr Brownlow had explained the form which was now held in the clipboard under Martin's increasingly sweaty arm. It was a series of 'tick boxes' and little spaces for comments which it was Martin's job to fill in.

Martin had to mark things like the sink in the kitchen (single drainer - tick - stainless steel - tick - mixer taps - tick) and count the eye-level cupboards and base cupboards and write down an answer.

While Mr Brownlow kept up his description of how Stiffhams would offer the house for sale and how it would be advertised and so on, Martin was dispatched upstairs to fill in the second part of his form, which involved counting wardrobes and radiators and that sort of thing.

The stairs rose to a little half-landing from the small hallway which, Martin noticed, was painted entirely in white, as were all the rooms he had seen so far. Other than the ghastly thing filling one wall in the lounge, there were no other pictures and somehow Martin felt that although the day was quite warm, this house had a bit of a chill to it.

As he turned the corner and arrived at the first floor landing Martin noticed, and ticked the box for the loft access hatch, and opened the first door on his left.

This was the smaller of the two bedrooms with a window looking towards the road and Martin was surprised to see that it contained no furniture at all except a long, wide, white sofa. The very same sofa which appeared in the enormous painting downstairs.

Having ticked his boxes, Martin rapidly moved on to the next door, which was the unremarkable workmanlike bathroom, relieved only by every surface being covered by little bottles and pots containing all sorts of lotions and potions, interspersed by several partly burnt candles.

Martin ticked his boxes and moved on to the next room.

This, of course, was the 'master bedroom' in Estate Agent speak, and Martin cringed when on the wall behind the bed, a smaller, and mercifully less revealing version of the picture downstairs smote his eye.
At least, this time the model was draped in a bathrobe, but those penetrating eyes were now in a face that had the same slightly terrifying smile Miss Pendle had given him in the lounge.
The awful painting seemed to hold a message for him, saying it was all right to look; so Martin concentrated hard on his tick boxes and tried not to glance at it again.

The final door on the landing was just at the top of the stairs and to open it Martin had to move a small chair out of the way.

There wasn't much space between this door and the stairs and it opened outwards so Martin had to step backwards towards the top step to open it. The door was tight in its frame and Martin had to give it quite a tug to get it to open.

As it came open, with something of a rush, everything seemed to happen at once.

With a screech, an enormous tabby cat shot out of

the cupboard at about the level of Martin's face and an avalanche of blankets and pillows and clothes burst from the shelves.

Martin stepped back, missed his footing on the top step and fell helter-skelter down the stairs.

The noise, of course, brought Miss Pendle and Mr Brownlow running, and as they arrived Martin, though dazed, saw that he still had his pen clutched firmly in his hand.

All down the wall in great arcs perfectly describing his fall, there was now a line of blue ink on the otherwise unmarked paintwork.

The blankets, pillows and clothes had served to break Martin's fall to some extent and apart from a few bruises to his pride, Martin was pretty much undamaged.

Of the tabby cat, that actually lived next door, little more can be said. It charged into the lounge as Mr Brownlow and Miss Pendle came out and presumably shot out of the cat-flap in the kitchen that Martin had so assiduously noted on his form.

As Mr Brownlow and Miss Pendle helped him to his feet, however, he could not take his eyes off the pen-line all down the wall and he burned with embarrassment as he stammered out an apology.

Miss Pendle saw what he was looking at, and in the

long seconds that followed, Martin and Mr Brownlow stood and stared.

Then quite suddenly Miss Pendle threw back her head and released a throaty, rolling laugh that shook the walls and was so infectious and went on for so long that Mr Brownlow soon joined in. Even Martin managed an embarrassed sheepish grin before remembering his manners and offering to clean up the damaged wall himself, if Miss Pendle would find that sufficient recompense for his clumsy accident.

As they were leaving, Miss Pendle explained that the enormous tabby cat liked to use this house as its headquarters when its own people were at work and loved to sneak into the airing cupboard to snooze in the warm, especially in the winter months. She went on to say that she had not seen the cat for several days and wondered how long it had been there.

That mystery was to remain unresolved, however, as Mr Brownlow having finished photographing the house, packed away his cameras and made ready to leave.

-oOo-

The estate agent's window, set as it was in a little parade of shops just off the high street, saw only limited footfall.

Those who did stop were usually either genuine buyers or husbands waiting for wives visiting the dress shop next door.

One such husband was Geoffrey. His interest however was piqued by a photograph in the window of one of those houses on that popular estate that he had always rather liked.

'New on,' the banner across one corner of the picture proclaimed, and Geoffrey's eye took in 'immaculate order, large garden, garage and driveway' in the effusive description.

Geoffrey glanced through the window of the dress shop.

As far as he could make out, his wife must be in the fitting room, so would be ages yet.

He grasped the handle of the estate agent's door and stepped inside.

Steve had been watching Geoffrey from his desk inside the office and the view afforded between the plastic picture-hangers of the street outside enabled him to form an opinion of those who looked in the window or, when nobody was there, to watch the pretty girls on their way to the railway station beyond.

Steve thought that Geoffrey looked harassed. One of those men with domineering wives who made their lives a misery, he thought.

'Good morning,' he said as Geoffrey edged furtively through the door.

-oOo-

Of course, with no driving licence, let alone a car, Martin could not drive the customers around himself yet, as Steve and his other colleagues might. But sometimes Martin got to accompany potential buyers in their own cars.

Steve thought that was handy, especially if he wanted to be on his own in the office, as sometimes suited him.

Martin sat uncomfortably in the back of Geoffrey's car as Geoffrey's wife roundly told him off for wasting her time. She did not want to view houses, she informed him, and was annoyed that he had 'high-handedly' made this appointment. It was too late now, they were nearly there, but Geoffrey cowered over the steering wheel and Martin squirmed on his seat as the tirade went on.

Strictly speaking, Steve did not need to send Martin or anyone from the offices of Stiffhams Estate Agents to accompany viewers to 2 Easton Drive. The vendor there was quite happy to show people round and perfectly capable of dealing with Geoffrey and his hectoring wife, but Steve and Martin were on their own in the office this morning and Steve seized the opportunity to be completely alone to make a furtive telephone call and make plans with Rosalind, while her husband was at work. Martin did not know Steve's motivation, of course and in his keen way he was just delighted to be doing something to help a possible sale.

When they arrived Martin introduced everyone and started the house tour with an obvious and unnecessary observation that this was the entrance hall.

Geoffrey looked at his wife and then, when he was sure she wasn't looking at him, he glanced again at Janet. He liked what he saw very much indeed.

Miss Janet Bassett BDS, MSc was, to Geoffrey's eyes at least, absolutely gorgeous.

Her lustrous brown hair, large bright eyes and incredible smile reminded some people of a faithful Labrador, but to Geoffrey she was adorable in a quite different way.

When she smiled, her perfect teeth glowed as if she had swallowed a pocket torch and were the result of a considerable investment which, even at staff rates, came at an eye-watering price. The dental practice where Janet worked, however, were justifiably proud of their efforts and regularly produced Janet as an example of what they could achieve to customers. She had even been professionally photographed and most of her face now graced the practice's printed advertising material.

To Geoffrey, quite unaware of all this dental work, she was just about flawless and he was having trouble dragging his eyes from her long enough to give 2 Easton Drive the attention it deserved.

Not so Geoffrey's wife, whose critical eye took in every detail of the house, and was not particularly impressed.

As Martin's unnecessary comments explaining the function of each room lagged just a little behind the rapid inspection she was giving it, before she moved on, it was obvious that she wanted the viewing over and done with as quickly as possible, so she could return to berating her husband for wasting her time.

Martin was not immune to the tension in the air. He saw and understood the disinterest Geoffrey's wife was exhibiting as his hopes for a share of Steve's commission on the sale were dashed. But he also noticed something else.

Geoffrey was gazing at Janet and to his surprise, Janet was returning his stare with little smiles and exhibiting a slight blush around the temples.
Martin had seen that sort of thing between boys and girls at his school and had a fair idea what it meant, so teaming up with Geoffrey's wife now, he hurried the house inspection on and bought the visit to a conclusion as fast as he could.

The journey back to the office to drop Martin off was conducted in a sort of strained silence.
Martin hopped out of the car and with only the minimum of polite comments, scuttled back into the office as soon as they arrived.

'Well,' said Steve, 'What happened?'

-oOo-

They met again in Waitrose by chance, and after

that there were stolen dinners, when Geoffrey lied to his wife about a dinner at the golf club, and long telephone calls.

The subterfuge deepened when Geoffrey, who volunteered part time for a housing charity, invented a three day conference in Leeds. They were always wanting him to attend seminars and conferences so his wife was not suspicious; but he and Janet actually spent the time in Brighton, almost entirely closeted in their hotel.

Geoffrey knew his life had changed forever when Janet took his destiny in her hand and gently rolled back his resistance. Six weeks later Geoffrey was observed leaving the solicitors' offices opposite Stiffhams Estate Agents where he had been arranging to start divorce proceedings.
He gave his address at that meeting as 2 Easton Drive.

-o0o-

Rosalind realised she had been very foolish, of course.

She should never have encouraged Steve, and now she was finding it hard to shake him off.

He may be tall and handsome and certainly charming, but she was happily married, wasn't she? All right, she and Mike had been having this on-going rumbling row for about six weeks now, and she couldn't even remember what started it, but harsh words had been exchanged and sniping, niggling comments had coloured their conversations ever since.

Mike was great though. Solid dependable Mike. Straightforward uncomplicated Mike. What ever was the matter with her? Why on earth had she allowed Steve to buy her that drink? It was foolish and impulsive and, although that was as far as it went, Steve obviously thought she was still interested and was pushing to take her out to dinner and God knows what.

Even if she wanted to, how on earth could she do that? She had Mike's supper to cook and she never went out on her own anyway. Why would she?

She was going to tell Steve to leave her alone and she knew she would have to do it soon.

Rosalind was under no illusions as to what lay behind her problems. She and Mike had been trying for a baby on and off for ages, There was nothing wrong with either of them and they had been for all the tests and tried all the usual medical things, including IVF, but it made no difference. Something was stopping them starting a family.
Then recently it seemed Mike had lost interest in her altogether and she was feeling rather unloved.

Rosalind wanted the typical family and they had worked out that even just on Mike's salary, they could fairly comfortably afford the typical modest family house. That was how she met Steve.

She went into the estate agent's offices when she saw a picture of a really nice little house in the window, just to find out a bit more about it, and somehow Steve had got her to put her name on their mailing list.

When the property details started arriving, Mike had gone ballistic. She should have talked to him about it, of course she should; but this rolling unhappy row got in the way. What a mess!

The flat was a mess, too.

After she was made redundant she had no excuse not to keep their home immaculate.

She stirred herself and went to wash out her coffee cup. She was usually so house proud and almost obsessive about keeping it all clean and tidy, but since this silly row started she knew she had let it slide.

Rosalind sank back down on the sofa and cried.

-oOo-

As he was coming out of the offices of Oakshott, Parslow & Partners, Solicitors and Commissioners for Oaths, Geoffrey held the door open for Sylvia Pendle, who was on her way in.

On Mr Brownlow's recommendation, Sylvia had come to instruct these solicitors in the matter of the sale of her house, and had an appointment to see their Mrs Pauline Patrick, who was to act on her behalf.

Sylvia did not know it of course, but Mrs Patrick had recently been promoted to the position as Head of Conveyancing, on the retirement of old Mr Shotter, who had held the post for over twenty years.

Mrs Patrick had been with Oakshott, Parslow & Partners, for fifteen of those years, just waiting and hoping for this moment and, now that it had arrived, she had decided to make some sweeping changes to modernise the conveyancing department from the ground up.

She had started by offering the post of 'Trainee Paralegal' to Dawn DeSantos, who left school at the same time as Martin Dartnell-Parkes, although Dawn did have an 'A' level and several more GCSEs than Martin could boast.

Oakshott, Parslow & Partners, had snapped her up as the most promising of what, it must be said, was a pretty ordinary bunch of school leavers this year.

Dawn was a decorative girl, with rather lovely fingernails which she filed almost continuously as she sat at the smaller of the two desks in the outer office of the Conveyancing Department, waiting for something to happen.

When Mr Shotter retired, Helen, the department's secretary resigned and went to work at Waitrose. Until a replacement was found, Dawn DeSantos was expected, amongst her other duties (such as they were) to meet and greet visitors to the department and show them through to Mrs Patrick's office.

Dawn knew Sylvia Pendle from school, of course, and had attended her 'literature appreciation' sessions in the library in her last two terms there, so she was able to greet her warmly.

The Conveyancing Department, it has to be said, had not been especially busy for the last few months and old Mr Shotter's attempts to drum up business had not been a great success. As a result, the firm had had to let the other conveyancing clerk go, and the full weight and burden of the entire portfolio of work now fell just to Mrs Patrick, with assistance from Dawn DeSantos when she was not on one of her two days a week at college training to be a Paralegal.

That said, apart from the need to appoint a secretary/receptionist, the department was not what one might call understaffed. The burden of existing cases could best be described as 'light' and Mrs Patrick had been delighted to be able to offer her services to Ms Sylvia Pendle, in the matter of the sale of her house.

While Dawn made the tea, Mrs Patrick cleared her desk and opened discussions, as she always did with a new client, by explaining the fees payable.

-oOo-

Mr Brownlow was late.

Mr Brownlow was never late, well, not until today anyway. Martin stood by the front door ready to go.

It was kind of Mr Brownlow to give Martin a lift to work. It had started because it was raining really heavily on Martin's first day at Stiffhams, and Mr Brownlow had offered to drop Martin home when the office closed. Because it was still raining the next day, Mr Brownlow also picked him up and the arrangement had sort of rolled on from there. As Mr Brownlow had to drive past the end of Martin's road, it did not inconvenience him unduly and certainly suited Martin.

Tomorrow Martin would have his eighth driving lesson.
He couldn't wait to pass his driving test and be able to drive to work. He had no car, of course, but he was saving up.

It helped that his father paid for the driving lessons and there had been vague discussions about helping Martin to buy a car one day. For now though, Martin could either walk to work, ride his rickety bicycle, or continue to rely on Mr Brownlow's generosity in giving him lifts.

At last the sleek BMW pulled up outside, but Mr Brownlow was getting out.

'Could I just wash my hands, Martin? I had a flat tyre and had to put the spare on and I got a bit dirty,' he said.

Martin showed Mr Brownlow to the downstairs cloakroom just as his mother came out of the kitchen.

'Good morning, Mrs Dartnell-Parkes. Apologies for the inconvenience,' he added.

Martin rapidly explained what had happened and

hoped his mother wouldn't want to chat. He wanted to get to work, where life seemed so much more interesting.

Mr Brownlow was always very polite and thanked Martin and his mother for letting him wash his hands with a smile.

'We had better be getting along, young Martin. It doesn't do to be late to the office.'

'Yes, Mr Brownlow,' said Martin automatically. He was relieved that his mother's opportunity to chat had been stifled before she had the chance to start.

Martin's mother was a great one for a chat and in his youth, when Martin was obliged to accompany her to the shops, it had taken what seemed like hours to even get there. His mother always stopped to speak to everyone she met along the way; and callers to the house usually had to submit to lengthy chatting before they got away.

Safely in Mr Brownlow's car now, Martin sighed in relief.

'Today, Martin, we are going to spend a little time on telephone technique, so that you know what to say to the customers and so that you can start to deal with enquiries.'

Martin thought Mr Brownlow must have read his mind. How, he had been wondering, could he start to earn commission if he didn't know what to say to the customers to get them to buy the houses?

'But you will have to excuse me for a little while when we get to the office as I need to get hold of the company that lease this car. I need to tell them about the puncture and discuss changing my car for a new one.'

'This is a very nice car, Mr Brownlow,' said Martin.

'Yes, but it is very expensive to run and it is nearly four years old now. I'm thinking of getting something more economical.'

Four years didn't seem very long to own a car to Martin. He supposed any car he would be able to buy himself would probably be much older, possibly ten or even twenty years old. Mr Brownlow, Martin decided, must make lots of commission to be able to change his car after just four years, and he wondered again about how soon *he* would start earning commission.

-o0o-

Dawn DeSantos was proud of her 'A' level.

She had obtained a good grade and had put the little certificate in a plastic frame, which previously contained a picture of her long-departed pony. It sat now on her dressing table, alongside all the paraphernalia she needed to keep her fingernails in such good order.

Her boyfriend (soon to be ex-boyfriend), had told her

she was fixated and spent far too much time messing about with her nails.

He didn't have an 'A' level though, so Dawn regarded him now as her social inferior and she had decided it was time he was added to the list of those whom Dawn had consented to date, but had been cast aside when they did not come up to scratch.

She could do much better, she thought. She was looking for a real man this time. Someone who was kind certainly, but much less like … like a boy. Someone more mature than the previous pretenders to the throne.

Someone who looked like that bloke from the estate agent's opposite the office, perhaps. He was tall and strong looking with a broad chest and he wore quite tight suit trousers.

She had never actually spoken to him, of course, and now she came to think about it, he was probably some oily, snaky type who didn't tell the truth - all estate agents were like that, according to her father.

Maybe not him then, but someone who looked bit like him at least.

That ginger-nob, Martin, from school, who got a job there thought the world of him. But Martin, while sweet in his way, was just another boy who knew nothing of the ways of the world.

When the telephone on her desk rang, the surprise meant Dawn just stared at it for a moment as the reverie she had been enjoying melted away and the reality of life in the solicitor's office returned.

On the second ring she lifted the instrument and, as she had been instructed, said 'Conveyancing, Dawn speaking, how may I help you?'

-oOo-

Chapter 2

Bryn Williams might have been the only painter she had ever met who had actually managed to sell any of his paintings, but regardless of any monetary value they may have, Sylvia Pendle hated them all.

Now she had a hammer.

She tucked it into the elasticated waistband of her pale grey track suit and manhandled the massive canvas from the lounge out into the garden.

There, she set about it with the hammer until the frame splintered and broke and the canvas hung in shreds. Then, one after the other, she struck three matches to get it going and burned the wretched thing.

That, she noted with satisfaction, was the last time Bryn Williams talked her out of her clothes and the naked, stark, white wall in the living room where the enormous and offensive picture had hung could not now distract any potential purchasers viewing the house.

As the flames started to die down Sylvia remembered something and ran upstairs.

She snatched the smaller portrait from behind the bed and, pausing only to grab two books from one of the bookcases, she added the second Bryn Williams portrait to the fire.

Struggling now not to laugh out loud, Sylvia threw the books into the flames.
First Bryn's battered copy of the ghastly Karma Sutra, and then with a determined swing, his copy of 'Fifty Shades Of Grey'.

She could contain the laughter no more, however, when the second book struck the part of the stylised portrait on what was supposed to be her bottom. The irony of that made the rumbling, throaty laugh she had been holding back burst from her like air out of a balloon.

Sylvia Pendle was free at last.
Free to call herself Sylvia Pendle, not Mrs Bryn Williams, and she intended to make the most of it.

-oOo-

Solid dependable Mike sat at his desk with his head in his hands.

How had it come to this? He had a good job with reasonable prospects, and the only girl in the world had consented to marry him despite, no doubt, receiving almost hourly proposals from far more eligible suitors.

Something had changed however when Rosalind (never Ros; that wouldn't do) was made redundant.
Mike thought she might be blaming herself again for losing her job, although it was hardly her fault that she had only been there three years and all the other employees seemed to have joined when the place was built during the reign of Queen Victoria.
'Last in, first out' was a well established principle in these matters, and he had told Rosalind so repeatedly.

No, there was something else. Something was eating away at his lovely girl, and the snapping, cutting comments they exchanged on a daily basis now only made it worse.

There was the baby thing, of course. But that had been an issue for a good twelve months before the redundancy, so was nothing new. Mike felt awful about that, of course, but after all the tests, failed treatments and what-not they had been through he thought Rosalind had come to terms with it.

Mike still hoped there might be a solution, however, and had been on the internet again looking for new ideas. If he could find something new that would finally give her the baby she so wanted, he would try it in a heartbeat.

Maybe this latest thing some American-Indian quack-doctor proposed was worth a try. All he had to do was withdraw his services for two or three months so that his potency would build up a head of steam. The lack of action might make Rosalind a bit more randy too, he thought, which was all to the good.

He had attempted on several occasions to explain this new plan to Rosalind, but every time he tried, this dragging row about ... he couldn't remember ... would raise its head again and they would start biting each others' heads off.

Mike loved Rosalind with every fibre of his being. He knew she wanted to nest now, she had even been looking for a house, but he couldn't break the circle of despair they seemed to be falling into.

Mike reached for the telephone. Maybe if he suggested they went to view that nice little house Rosalind had been talking about, it would help.

-oOo-

Miss Janet Bassett BDS, MSc, said goodbye to her last patient of the day and peeled off her latex gloves.

She was looking forward to her evening with Geoff (as she called him) when they would be driving over to a nearby town to meet some of her friends.
Unusually, in such a situation, Janet felt no concerns about these introductions. She knew she had her old friends support and she had not hesitated to tell them how she felt about Geoff.

Geoff, or Geoffrey (as we knew him), sat outside the

dental practice in his Jaguar.

The plan was to take Janet home to get ready for their date and, now that all Geoff's clothes were also at 2 Easton Drive, for him to change there too.

Geoff (I think we had better call him Geoff from now on) was less comfortable about meeting these new people. He had loved having Janet all to himself and had become increasingly relaxed in her company.

There was no doubt that he was a new man since moving into 2 Easton Drive. He was fitter, slimmer, healthier and above all much, much happier. But he felt an irrational fear about sharing Janet, even with her old friends and, perhaps understandably was all too aware that tonight he was on show.

Janet had bought him some new chinos and a smart new shirt and these lay ready on the bed for the evening ahead. She had explained that it would be a relaxed affair, with drinks at Lucy's before they all moved on to the restaurant for dinner.

Lucy, it emerged, was Janet's closest college friend who, also married to a dentist, had been at university with several of those expected to turn up tonight.

Geoff was unclear about the numbers involved, but worried that these old college re-unions could get a bit much and he may be left out of things.

He didn't mind that so much and, as his wife had regularly accused him of having "not much conversation" anyway, he expected to be on the edges of the discussions, but he did hope Janet wouldn't abandon him with a bunch of people he didn't know.

Janet looked fabulous, of course, and Geoff wondered, as he often did, if their age difference showed too much. It was only ten years, but it put him in a bracket where, if they started talking about television programmes they remembered, for example, they would quickly leave him with no idea what they were talking about.
He mentioned this now as they drove towards the event.

'No, Geoff,' Janet replied, 'I don't suppose we will talk about television programmes, so you won't feel out of it. The conversation usually reaches a higher level than that. These are all comfortably-off successful people with good careers, marriages and children. It's only me, left on the shelf, who had time to sit about watching the telly.'

Geoff felt in his pocket for his indigestion tablets. He had a feeling he might be needing them tonight.

-o0o-

As Martin ended his conversation on the telephone with Miss Pendle, he had a broad smile on his face.

He had just made his first 'appointment to view' from start to finish. He had correctly recorded the relevant details in the much prized 'Viewing Book'; which apparently was admissible evidence in Court so had to be assiduously kept up to date, although Martin was a little shaky on what that meant or why it mattered so much.

Admittedly there had been some discussion in the office about legal precedents in cases of disputes between agents and so on relating to this book, but Martin had not really been paying attention.

He had, however, accurately entered all the details on the computer and agreed the date and times with the prospective purchasers, as they were called, and the seller alike, switching between two phone lines without cutting anybody off or any of the other accidents he had been warned could so easily occur.

'Well done, Martin,' said Mr Brownlow, who had been watching proceedings incase he needed to step in.
'Now, if they make an offer you can sit in on the negotiations with Steve or me and see how it is done.'

Martin was getting somewhere now, he thought.

'And, if a sale results which goes through, we shall see about some commission for you out of it.'

Martin's grin widened. Commission at last! He couldn't wait.

-oOo-

Geoff turned into the swish private road of widely spaced, detached houses each with gates and broad sweeping drives.

'It's this one,' said Janet, although it was obvious a gathering of some sort was taking place because the drive was overflowing with Porsches, Range Rovers and Mercedes, and the substantial house beyond shed light from every window.

Geoff noticed, to his dismay, that his Jaguar, bought secondhand in a moment of wild rebellion five years ago, much to the irritation of his wife, was probably ten years older than any of the other cars on the impressive driveway.

His disquiet deepened still further when he saw how many cars there were. It was clear this was going to be quite a large event.

Ever the old school gentleman, Geoff rushed round to open the door for Janet when they parked and was rewarded for his trouble by one of her dazzling smiles.

'Don't worry, I'm sure that you will enjoy yourself once you relax; and I promise,' she said, offering her hand, 'that the rather nicely manicured hand in yours will be mine. I won't stray far from your side.'

'Thank you, Janet,' he said as another radiant smile beamed upon him.

-oOo-

As Sylvia swept the ashes off the little patio after her joyful fire, she remembered some of the indignities she had suffered with Bryn Williams.

The two books had not really burned much, she should have torn them up first perhaps, so she popped them in a plastic bag and consigned them to the dustbin. But at least the frightful portraits had gone from her life forever now.

Bryn had painted them both soon after they moved into this little house, she recalled. He was trying, he said, to recapture a period in their lives when they visited a particularly unpleasant nudist colony in Wales.

Sylvia had been dead against the idea of that trip, but Bryn wheedled away at it and got round her in the end as he always seemed to do.

Bryn knew some artist who had been there before who told him it was where some famous rock band had held a retreat in the late 1960s or early 1970s. By the mid 1980s however it was a collection of bleak, cold huts and tents with intermittent plumbing and a rotten tennis court with a puddle in the middle of it.

Bryn had been a closet nudist for years and regularly wandered about in the buff when they were at home. Sylvia needed more convincing to shed her clothes and loathed every second of the four days in early June they spent on that breezy Welsh hillside.

Yet it was a different Welsh hillside she was drawn to now. When the house was sold, she had decided she would join a writers' club in North Wales that had leased a crumbling country house as a quiet place for writers and those of a literary mindset to regain their equilibrium away from the noise of modern life.

She had visited for a long weekend to see if she liked it and soon found herself in animated conversation with an eclectic mix of people from all walks of life. She had felt instantly at home.

She was looking forward particularly to seeing Margaret again, one of the organisers and a director of the little company the club had formed to take out the lease on the rambling old house. Margaret wrote wonderful stories of life in her native Ireland, and Sylvia had now read all her published books.

Then, amongst the residents, there was David. Round and jolly with an enormous beer gut and a wealth of stories of his life travelling the world chasing his dreams. Laughter was never far away when in conversation with him. And there was young moody, slightly withdrawn Shaun. Clearly from a posh family, who indulged and funded his 'need to write', as he put it.

Sylvia thought that perhaps the family just wanted him out of the way, although she was not sure about him yet, but was going to enjoy finding out about him, and the dozen or so other residents at the comfortable house.

She hoped this young couple who were due to come round liked her house. It was ideal for a young family. Far more suitable than it had been for Bryn and Sylvia.

Sylvia would be glad to be away from it and all the memories it held.

-oOo-

Cutting the call on her mobile phone, Dawn DeSantos allowed herself a satisfied smile.

Ditching Pete had been easy although, of course, she had just imagined that he seemed quite cheerful about it. No doubt that was just an act to cover his embarrassment. He was such a child.

Dawn didn't actively dislike Pete, but she couldn't say she actually liked him either. He was just another boy who she had met since leaving school, and now he was history.

At college, where she went two days a week, the corridors were stalked by a much more sophisticated type of male. Blokes with 'A' levels who had prospects. On Tuesday, when she went there again, she would have more of a look at the talent on display and see if any of it came up to her exacting specifications .

Tuesday. That reminded her. She had a mountain of reading to get through before the next class, and she had been rather neglecting it.

With a sigh she put down her nail file, reached for her books and lay face down on the bed with her feet in the air to dry the varnish on her toenails.

-oOo-

Chapter 3

Geoff was introduced to Lucy first and was immediately handed a glass of fizzy wine.

Lucy, and almost everyone at the house had a spectacular set of teeth which glowed as if illuminated by some hidden source when they smiled. The world of dentistry, previously a closed book to Geoff, was populated by smiling rich people, it seemed.

The trappings of unashamed wealth were everywhere, from the designer handbags carelessly placed on chairs to the glittering jewellery hung on wrists of men and around the necks of the stylishly dressed females he was introduced to.

Geoff had prepared a little line to say which he felt dealt neatly with the two challenges he might face. To each new person he proposed to say,
'Lovely to meet you. Now I do hope you will forgive me if I muddle your name up as the evening progresses. I'm frightful at remembering names. It's probably my age.'
He proposed to follow this with a little chuckle

and a winning smile and hoped it would deflect embarrassing questions and give him chance to change the subject away from himself.

If he did forget their names after that, so what? He had already apologised for that.

He actually only got to use his little line once, to Lucy. The next person he was introduced to was an elderly Sri-Lankan dentist named Sennijaritheran or something like that; and his pre-prepared face saver would to have been inappropriate and may even have caused offence.

This wizened little man, he assumed, was Lucy's boss as she introduced him as 'The Senior Partner'. He flashed Geoff the inevitable luminous smile and said 'How do you do?'

Bereft of his safety line, Geoff was adrift.

How *did* he do? How did he do what? How do you answer such an odd question?

Geoff could not say he was all right apart from a mild toothache or the place would have erupted and he would have found himself held down in a reclining chair as a myriad of brightly smiling dentists revved up their drills.

In the end he mumbled some platitude and took a sip of his fizzy wine.

The introductions seemed to go on for ever and he soon had to let go of Janet's hand to accept a canapé from a tray which was being offered around.

He had thought about this contingency and had a plan ready. He had decided only to accept a canapé if he could choose one which could be eaten easily in one mouthful and didn't look as if it would fall apart as soon as he touched it.

He chose a little bit of dry toast with something that turned out to be some sort of fishy toffee on it. He did his best to chew it up, but the glutinous topping seemed to take some time to give up the fight.

Perhaps, he thought, this was a special sort of canapé for dentists to try out their artificially enhanced teeth. Certainly his standard issue natural ones had a bit of a fight to dispose of the item and when, at last, he gulped it down and unstuck the final bit of the horribly sticky stuff from the roof of his mouth, he found to his dismay that a tall woman with a gold necklace and bright red lipstick framing her glowing white teeth, had just asked him 'How do you do?' and was standing in front of him expecting an answer.

-oOo-

Martin couldn't sleep that night.

He tossed and turned and worried about how his 'applicants', as they were called, had got on when they viewed Miss Pendle's house.

His principle fear of course was that the ghastly nude portrait, with the staring eyes filling up half the lounge wall, would immediately send them scurrying back to their car to recover from the shock.

His sleep would have been less disturbed if he had known about the jolly little bonfire which had taken place the night before.

When, at two thirty, he went downstairs for a glass of cold milk and encountered his mother in the kitchen on a similar mission, he was glad for once to sit and chat with her and told her all about the revolting picture.

'Some people,' pronounced Mrs Dartnell-Parkes over the breakfast table later that morning, 'have no sense of what is fitting.' She went on to say that it would serve this Miss Pendle right if she couldn't sell her house. 'Displaying upsetting and possibly pornographic images in the living rooms of suburban semi-detached houses is simply not done,' she declared frostily.

Martin was too tired and bleary eyed to correct her by explaining that Miss Pendle's was an end-of-terrace rather than a semi-detached house, and he munched his cereal in silence.

-oOo-

Mrs Pauline Patrick, Legal Executive, looked around at the familiar and comfortable setting of Mr Shotter's office.

It was her office now, of course, but she automatically

thought of it in those terms because for the previous fifteen years it was Mr Shotter who proprietorially enjoyed this view.

The solid English oak desk had an inlaid leather panel which was once a smart green with gold detailing around the edges. It was faded now and one of the drawers was stuck shut, but it still served its purpose. The funny old flip over date thing sat, as it always had, telling the staff the month, day of the week and date; so long as someone remembered to alter it each day, of course.

On the broad mahogany fireplace the green marble mantle clock gently ticked away the hours as it had so faithfully done since long before even Mr Shotter's time; so long as someone wound it up every day. Winding it had been one of Pauline's jobs when she first joined the firm.

The clean white blotter was in place along with the onyx pot with the spare pens. The intriguing, antique, rotary pencil sharpener was attached to the desk edge and the two wire baskets sat on the left and right of the occupant of the old wood and leather 'Captain's chair' as usual.

Mrs Patrick crossed the threadbare carpet and, looking past the wooden coat stand and the ancient safe, stared out of the grimy sash window at the car park.

It would all have to go, of course.

Mrs Patrick envisaged a glass meeting table with

white leather chairs and a big screen for conference calls. There would be a smart desk at one end with a docking station for her laptop and two screens so she could read documents while watching her emails update at the same time. But first, the Partners had made clear, the Conveyancing Department had to start to pay its way and the recent slow-down in the property market, along with the effect of interest rates and the cost-of-living increase had not made new business easy to come by.

Alone in the department now, Pauline Patrick, Legal Executive and newly appointed Head of Conveyancing wondered what she was going to do about it.

She disliked being on her own in the office when Dawn was at college and now that the familiar clatter of the secretary's keyboard had ceased, not that there was much to type anyway at present, it was too quiet. The Conveyancing Department was not the hive of activity it had once been.

She would chase up that employment agency, she decided. They must have had some applicants for the receptionist/secretarial post they were advertising by now. She could at least usefully spend the time until the next client arrived interviewing people for that job.

-oOo-

Everything was ready to the last spoon and napkin, but Antonio went round the tables one last time to check.

This dinner was a big booking for the restaurant and it was important to get everything right, which was why he had taken personal charge of the arrangements.

Flicking an invisible speck of dust from an irreproachable linen tablecloth, Antonio DeSantos was excited as well as a little nervous.

Fifty-two covers was a big deal for his business and shutting the restaurant for the evening for a private party like this was not without its risks.

He had called in all his staff, temporary as well as permanent, to lend a hand; he even had family members working in the kitchen to ensure everything went smoothly.

Well, most family members, anyway. His surly daughter Dawn refused to have anything to do with this, the third generation of the family business, preferring her crazy ideas for some other career.

Whatever was a 'Paralegal', he thought. Some solicitor who arrives in Court by parachute in a full gown, wig and army boots?

Antonio had no idea what she was playing at.

And after, he mused, her grandmother, his own mother, had taught her all the old recipes herself before she died! His only daughter bought shame to the family.

Her and her 'A' level!

What would his grandfather, the first Antonio, have made of it? After all his sacrifices when, as Anton Walters he had escaped from Austria and changed his name from Anton to Antonio to avoid any Germanic inferences being drawn, and then from Walters to DeSantos when the Jewish motif was unpopular, and it suited better to claim he was a refugee from Franco's fascist Spain.

After all his work to set up what was then just a humble cafe! And then his own father, the second Antonio, who worked night and day to build up the business into a flourishing respectable restaurant. What would he have thought of Dawn's intransigence?

And now, thought Antonio, as the third generation head of the family, this, tonight! A nine-course tasting menu for fifty-two paying guests at over £50 a head! What a dynasty Antonio's had become.

How proud old Anton would have been to see it now! And yet his one, his only, daughter would have nothing to do with it and would throw all that away for this legal parachuting nonsense!

Unconsciously Antonio snapped his fingers in dismay. Thinking some detail had been missed, his nephew, Stefano, was instantly at his side enquiring how he could serve.

He was a good boy, this Stefano, thought Antonio, as he instructed him to give one of the spotless glasses another polish.

'Aieee!' came the call from the front desk, 'The guests! They are arriving!'

Antonio drew in a slow, deep breath and walked to the entrance, just as the door was opened to admit first Lucy, then Geoff and Janet at the head of a stream of chattering wealthy dentists and their friends, who would swell the coffers of Antonio's restaurant very handsomely indeed.

-oOo-

Chapter 4

Mike knew the house was just right.

A little bleak at present perhaps, but Rosalind was a wonderful homemaker and would soon have it cosy and comfortable and ideal to welcome … to create a home for them both.

He had no need to ask how Rosalind felt about it. She was positively sparkling as they drove home in the car. The old Rosalind was back and at her best.

'Mike,' she said now, 'What do you think?'

'I love it,' said Mike honestly, 'and if I'm not mistaken, so do you.'

They decided that they must be very grown up when they got back to the flat and spend the evening working out their finances carefully and weighing up the pros and cons of such a big move.

'Coffee?' said Rosalind, skipping round the lounge on the tips of her toes when they got in.

'Rosalind …' growled Mike and, coffee and finances

forgotten, they headed straight to the bedroom.

The next morning their row was history and Mike was late for work.
Rosalind knew with almost complete certainty that something had changed and she was excited and felt better than she had done for weeks.

-oOo-

Every Wednesday after work, Mrs Pauline Patrick, Legal Executive and recently promoted Head of Conveyancing at Oakshott Parslow & Partners, Solicitors and Commissioners for Oaths, went to the nursing home to see her husband, Barry.

After the stroke there was some hope of a recovery, but now dementia set in and it was just a case of making him as comfortable as possible.

At first Pauline had railed at why nothing more was being done. Even though the Trust he had set up when he had a promising career in the City had continued to pay most of the nursing home's fees, she was still left with a not-inconsiderable bill every month to pay and she objected to paying just to have his laundry done and his pillows plumped.
Was there nothing they could do, she kept on asking, but the answer was always the same.

Pauline felt frustrated at first, and then as time went on, increasingly helpless.

Supposing, she thought, she had been the one

her bosses had chopped when the department was struggling. How would she have coped then?

The promotion to Head of Conveyancing would help a bit, she supposed. She had received a small increase in salary, but there had been talk of profit sharing if each department performed well and it had to be said that currently 'Conveyancing' was something of a drag on the finances of the firm.

With a sigh, Pauline pulled on her coat and set off once more to see if Barry recognised her this time.

-oOo-

Mike was tied up in meetings and, because he was late arriving for work he had much to catch up on and was in for a busy day, so he and Rosalind had agreed that she would call the agents.

Rosalind really should have made that call to tell Steve to back off before, and she knew it would be all the more awkward now.

She and Mike had agreed that they wanted to express serious interest in the house and see if there was room to negotiate the price down a bit, given that, as first time buyers, they had no property to sell and needed only to arrange a mortgage.

As Rosalind dialled the number she hoped it would be Steve who answered, so that she could make her position clear before they got down to business. She was excited to make the call because, of course, she wanted the house, but this thing with Steve did need to be cleared up, so she was also a little nervous.

'Stiffhams Estate Agents, Martin speaking,' said Martin as he answered the call, 'How may I help you?'

Rosalind hesitated. This was not how she hoped her conversation would start.

'Er .. hello,' she stammered. 'Is Steve there, please?'

'Yes certainly,' said Martin brightly. 'He is just finishing a call on the other line. Who shall I say is calling?'

Relieved, Rosalind gave her name and waited.

'It's them!' said Martin, efficiently putting the call on hold. 'My applicants from the viewing! She wants to speak to you, Steve.'

'Right-ho, Martin,' said Mr Brownlow. 'Put the call through but stay on the line so you can listen to how Steve handles the negotiations.'

'Hello?' said Steve.

'Steve? Look, it's Rosalind, and before you say anything I need you to know that it was very nice to have that drink with you and I was very flattered by what you said, but there cannot be anymore of this and there is no point in you keeping ringing me. I'm a happily married woman and I intend to stay that way, so please can we just be friends and keep it strictly business now?'

'Ah,' said Steve, looking at Martin and Mr Brownlow in quick succession.

Martin, he noticed, was bright red, and Mr Brownlow, who fortunately had not heard the incoming side of the conversation, was looking confused.

'Ah,' he repeated, 'Yes, of course. Just as you say. Of course. Yes. Erm … what did you think of the house you saw last night?'

-oOo-

At one point, when Janet was drawn off into conversation with another group and Geoff worried that he would be on his own, he was astonished to find there was someone at the party that he knew slightly.

'Hello, there,' said Clive, emerging from behind a forbidding looking German dentist who turned out to be his wife. 'Geoffrey, isn't it?'

Clive was one of the handful of commuters who became nodding acquaintances and then as the journey progressed, perhaps a little more pally, in the bar on the 17:21 out of Waterloo on a Friday evening.

Over cans of beer or gin and tonics, these stoic travellers shared their experiences of the privations of public transport in a spirit of mutual camaraderie.

Geoff discovered early on that Clive also worked in insurance in the City, although he was involved in life insurance, while Geoff worked in Commercial Reinsurance.

'Haven't seen you on the old train for a while,' he was saying now.

'No, well, the chance came up and I took early retirement three .. erm .. quite recently.'

'Sensible fellow,' said Clive. 'I'm fifty-five too in eighteen months and I'll be out of there like a shot when I get the chance. The only saving grace for me is the bar on the 17:21 on a Friday. You are lucky to be out of it.'

Geoff nodded in agreement. His wife had told him to retire at fifty-five in fact, and if not for that, as he had always rather enjoyed going to work, he would still be doing it now.

'Do you remember the chap from my firm who used to get off at the same stop as you on a Friday?'

Geoff wasn't sure.

'Old Barry Patrick. Splendid fellow. Used to drink scotch and carry The Sporting Life ...'

'Oh, ah,' said Geoff, none the wiser.

'Had a stroke two or three years ago now and hasn't been back since. He stayed up in town during the working week and used to organise little sporting and drinking evenings for those similarly placed. Much missed by the boys in the office, old Barry. I don't suppose, living in the same town, I mean, if you ever come across him, do you?'

Geoff had placed the commuter in question now. He was a bonhomous individual and on the train at least, was usually surrounded by a group of drinkers studying the form for the weekend's horse racing. Geoff had never seen him out of that environment although, as Clive said, they did both alight at the same railway station. On arrival, however, Barry headed for the Station Hotel while Geoff went straight home.

'I'd like to hear how he is and give him the best from the boys, so if you do stumble across him, do tell him to get in touch.'

At this point, and with mutual expressions of goodwill, Clive and his slightly brutal-looking wife moved off to talk to someone else, and Geoff was relieved to find Lucy was beginning to shepherd everyone to their cars to move on to the restaurant. Janet was beckoning to him from the hallway as coats were found and people began to prepare to leave.

-o0o-

Martin was left in no doubt what the threatening stare Steve was giving him meant.

When, as Mr Brownlow moved off to attend to a customer coming through the door, Steve put his index finger to his lips and then drew it across his neck, Martin understood that all right.

But he didn't understand what Steve was up to as he said he would call Rosalind back later about the matter, and ended the call.

'She might have been about to make an offer for Mrs Pendle's house …' he started to say.

'Leave it, Martin,' snarled Steve, 'Go and make some tea or something.'

Rosalind, whilst less confused at what had just happened, was frustrated that Steve wanted to call her back, and beyond saying that she liked it, she hadn't really had the chance to talk about the house or the viewing.

Not for the first time she wished that she had never encouraged Steve and that she had been able to finish it before they even viewed the house.

-oOo-

Sylvia Pendle would have liked to know what Rosalind and Mike thought of the house, too.

Such a nice young couple, she thought, and they did seem keen.

The chap from the estate agent had said they were 'first time buyers', so there would be no chain of interdependent sales if they were interested. That would suit Sylvia just fine. If she could avoid long and protracted negotiations it would reduce the amount of contact she would need to have with Bryn before she could get the mortgage paid off and his half of the remaining money paid over to him.

She knew what she planned to do with her share, but she wondered what Bryn was planning to do.

Probably get a flat or something with that sleazy baggage he had been sniffing around, she thought. Well, good luck to her and she was welcome to him!
Sylvia could not be certain but she had good reason to suspect that Bryn had taken up with the barmaid at the Station Hotel where he was staying when he first moved out.

He would be quite happy in a flea-pit like that, she thought and conjured up a mental picture of the crumbling Victorian pub, which was known for its peeling paint and sticky tables as much as the 'Z-list' washed-out bands and acts that occasionally performed there alongside the karaoke sessions they held once a month.

-oOo-

Pauline and Barry Patrick had been married for a little over eight years. They were very different and proved the old saying that opposites attract.

Pauline was bookish and quiet, and while working at the local solicitors', lived with her mother until the old lady died.
Barry, on the other hand, was a gregarious character with a little flat in London, where he spent the working week. He kept it on after they were married

so that he only had to tackle the often difficult commute at the beginning and end of each week.

He liked horse racing and regularly went to the bigger courses to indulge his passion. Pauline went with him a few times, but felt left out of it when Barry met up with his racing friends and got involved in drinking and loud laughing sessions at the bar, so she stopped going.

He seemed to lead a similar life in London, with pub friends to see in the evenings during the week, but his time spent with Pauline was very different.
They went to the cinema, joined the National Trust and went on little outings to the country for picnics or to see stately homes. But if they had no other plans, Barry tended his vegetables in a patch of garden at the back of Pauline's mother's house.

Barry told Pauline that he had no family, having grown up in foster care after a failed adoption. Their registry office wedding was attended only by Mr Shotter from work, acting as witness, and her mother, who at least saw her daughter married before she died a few months later.

They had met on a chilly railway station, when Pauline had to visit London for a training course. Barry had offered his umbrella when it suddenly started to snow and there was nowhere to shelter on the crowded platform.

They had dashed into the station buffet, where they

ordered tea and a revolting slice of sticky fruit cake and, as the bad weather meant successive trains were cancelled, they chatted until her train finally arrived and Barry asked for her phone number.

Pauline had spent the best years of her life mooning about after a teacher at the local school who, it turned out, preferred boys. Embarrassed, she had kept herself to herself after that, and expected to remain a spinster.
A romance in later life had not been anything she she was looking for or had expected, but she was glad it had happened.

The memories were hers to keep now as these days Barry, poor love, couldn't even remember his own name sometimes.

-oOo-

Chapter 5

Her carefully made up, manicured and fashionably dressed appearance did it of course.

Dawn DeSantos was an attractive girl at the best of times but she had made a special effort today, and the guys at the college had certainly not failed to notice her.

She had been asked out twice by lunchtime but was waiting to see if one particular person was going to make a move.

She found their eyes met regularly and, unlike the usual hungry looks she got from the randy young studs on the legal course, he seemed to be smiling slightly, as if something had amused him. As if, she imagined, he thought that, as a 'mature student', all this was a little beneath him, but he was prepared to go along with it for now.

He was undoubtedly handsome, in a 'Mr Darcy' sort of way, with dark brows and high cheek bones and a well-shaped jaw. His chest, she noticed, was quite broad and he must have been almost six foot tall, by her usually accurate observations. He was smartly dressed, too.

When he spoke, however, to answer the course leader's question, Dawn was surprised to find that he had an attractive accent. Was it Mediterranean? Italian? Spanish? Perhaps Mexican. She couldn't be sure, but it was very sexy and it certainly held her attention.

It took until the afternoon break for Dawn to manoeuvre herself into a position where he could talk to her, and initially she was disappointed that he was engaged in conversation with one of the lecturers who had taken the class earlier. When that conversation finished however, he looked at her from under lowered brows and seemed to smoulder as he said, 'The course, are you enjoying it, Dawn?'

She was somewhat surprised that he knew her name but she managed an appropriate reply and they began to slip through the gears of conversation, as she worked on him and moved to ensnare him.

There was no question about it, he was gorgeous and Dawn was going to enjoy making him fall for her.

-oOo-

'I wonder if I've had my lunch?' thought Barry.

Thoughts for him now seemed to come slowly, one by one, or all together in a jumbled rush. He found speech difficult sometimes, but his mind was in a whirl.

'Where have I put my keys? Is it teatime? I need the toilet,' he thought now, 'There's that noise again. My wife is coming? No, you are wrong, I'm not married. Have you seen my keys? What time is it? I must go, I've got to catch the 17:21. I need the toilet. Have I got my glasses on? Oh good, I was looking for those! Has the Sporting Life come yet? Hello … is that Janet? No; looks like her though … I never did tell Pauline about that. Where have I put my keys? No, I'm not married, I thought I told you that.'

Barry shook his head, but the jumble of thoughts continued unabated.

'I need the toilet. Did Janet ever realise what was going on? I must not miss the train. Is it dinner time yet? She paid for that insurance policy, silly girl. All those years. Thought she was my sister. Where are my glasses? Oh, hello, Vicar, you here again? Have some tea. Have you seen my keys by any chance?'

To anyone looking on, Barry's expression could constantly change and he made small noises or spoke an occasional sentence, but mostly he sat silently while the maelstrom of thoughts engulfed him.

'Years and years she paid into it. I got my commission each month, regular as clockwork. That made up for it a bit. I need the toilet. Sorry, I can't stop to talk, I'm going to Sandown Park. Is this stop Esher? Pauline? I don't know anyone called Pauline. Is it lunchtime yet? Hello, Vicar, have you seen the Sporting Life today? I didn't live in a nice house with my mother like Janet did, but I made her pay in the end. Years and years she paid into that policy, silly girl.'

Barry did have lucid moments, when he was here with the rest of us. He had one now.

'Do you know my wife's name, Vicar,' he said, 'I can't remember it. There is that noise again. Is this seat taken? It smells in here. Have you seen my keys?'

Then, as happened more often than not, he would fall into a fitful sleep until the next time.

Sometimes he would wake up shouting. Sometimes the staff had to sedate him and left him to sleep. Perhaps next time he wouldn't wake up at all.

Pauline held Barry's hand as the Vicar read out a prayer.

-oOo-

At last Rosalind got a call from Steve.

He apologised for the delay in getting back to her and explained he had wanted to be on his own when they talked and had to wait for the right moment.

'No you don't, Steve,' said Rosalind, 'There isn't a right moment. I told you earlier, there is nothing between us and never can be. I only called earlier to talk about the house we saw last night, but if you can't deal with it, I want to know who else I can talk to.'

'You are not going to mention anything to my boss about us, are you Rosalind?' Steve's voice held a note of concern.

'There was no "us", Steve, and it would be best if we never mentioned anything about it again,' said Rosalind firmly.

'Well, that is not the impression you gave me when you wore those tight jeans and sat running your foot up and down my leg.'

'I didn't!' squeaked Rosalind, 'If I touched your leg it was a pure accident and the result of the tables being too small in that cafe.'

'So there really is no hope for us, Ros?'

'Will you stop it, Steve! Or I *will* go and talk to your boss!'

'All right Ros, I'm only teasing. Message received.'

'And don't call me Ros, either.'

'Sorry .... So what *did* you think of that house last night?'

-oOo-

The meal, Geoff thought, was really quite pleasant.

He sat between Lucy and Janet so was protected, on two sides at least, from too much awkward polite chatter and the wrinkled old boy sitting opposite with the sixty-watt smile was very polite and made easy small talk.

Best of all, the meal consisted of a series of little tiny dishes with frequent pauses between them which gave his digestion ample time to deal with the rich food. He didn't need his tablets at all.

The little dishes were mostly very tasty, too. Granted one or two were not to his liking, but generally they were delicious and he had second helpings of several of them.

There was plenty of wine, but he was careful not to overdo it and drank fizzy water most of the time. When the food finally conked out and it was time to say goodnight he felt fine and was even relatively comfortable shaking all those hands again, now that nobody asked him that ludicrous "How do you do?" question and expected an answer.

In traffic, on the way back, Janet told him she knew he was nervous about it but he had coped very well.

It sounded like the sort of thing she said to her patients after some gruesome treatment in her dentist's chair, but she was smiling that fabulous smile of hers so he soon forgave her.

Possibly it was the relief of knowing that he had not done anything embarrassing or let her down, but whatever it was, as they sat at a red light, he reached for her hand, kissed it and before he could stop himself, he told her that he loved her.

-oOo-

Rosalind and Mike gathered up all the information they had been asked to bring along.

The mortgage broker chap would be at the agent's office at six o'clock and it meant Mike had to leave work early, but with any luck they would only have to do this once.

The agent said it would be wise to check the mortgage position before they actually made an offer and had set up a meeting with their 'in-house' mortgage broker.
Mike locked the door to the flat and Rosalind, struggling with a supermarket bag full of papers as well as her handbag, headed for the car.

Twenty-two year old Jonathan Ellis was an odious youth with a shiny suit and a company car which boasted a loud and strident stereo system. He roared up outside the agent's office, and ignoring the carpark around the back, killed the engine and the booming sound system as he pulled into the 'disabled' parking bay at the front.

Although the sun was setting, he checked that his expensive sunglasses were in just the right position on his head before grabbing his laptop and stepping out of the car.

Steve, who was giving Martin a lift home tonight so that Mr Brownlow could attend this meeting, was preparing to leave as he came through the door.

'S'aaap, Steve!' said Jonathan, or 'J' as he liked to be known, and offered Steve a high five.

'Hello, Jonathan,' replied Steve, barely able to conceal his distaste, 'Are you ready, Martin? Let's go.'

Martin's thirst for knowledge in his new profession meant that he would have liked to stay for this meeting and he felt very proprietorial about 'his' applicants, but Mr Brownlow explained that personal details would be discussed and the customer's privacy had to be protected, so Martin had to go.

'Where's old Brownpants?' Jonathan was saying now, 'I've got a red-hot date tonight with a right little raver, so I don't want to be here too long.'

'Mr Brownlow is in his office with the applicants now,' said Martin with some dignity.

'So knock first,' said Steve, 'and it might be an idea if you zip up your fly before you go in, J Man!'

'Eh?' said J and almost dropped his laptop as he fumbled with his trousers.

'Come on,' said Steve, ushering Martin out into the street with a wink and a grin.

-o0o-

Sylvia knew there was nothing definite yet and that the estate agent needed to do all their checks and what-not, but she had a good feeling about this.

The agent said Mike and Rosalind seemed keen and if details relating to mortgages and deposits could be confirmed, they might make an offer pretty soon.

On the strength of that she rang Margaret at the literary club's country house to give her an update.
It was lovely to hear her soft Irish accent again and Sylvia was impatient for all the 'due process' to be over so that she could immerse herself in her new life in Wales.

There is always a fly in the ointment, however, and Sylvia's seemed to be an answer phone message to call Bryn to discuss something to do with finances.

Sylvia knew, of course, that it would be a request for some money and that Bryn would say something along the lines of it being an advance on the money he was due on completion of the house sale. She had resisted making the call as long as she dared, but Bryn had a right to know what was going on with the sale of the house, and she knew she would have to call him.

She was saved the trouble however when her mobile rang and the screen showed that it was Bryn calling.

-oOo-

When Dawn got home from college she threw her bag across the room. What was the matter with men these days, she thought.

Things seemed to be going so well. Orlando had been polite and charming and she really thought … But something was holding him back and he didn't get to the point of asking her out before they were interrupted.

With a snarl that was most unbecoming in such a pretty girl, Dawn kicked her college bag across the kitchen floor and threw herself into an easy chair.

He was nice, though, she conceded and she could listen to that deep voice with its warm accent for ages. He had real prospects too, and was much further along the road to becoming a lawyer than the rest of the group.

Orlando was already qualified to practise as a conveyancer in his native Spain, where he worked for his father's law firm. The firm, he said, had offices in Madrid, Marbella, Alicante and more recently London and Germany. He was at the college because his father had sent him to become qualified to practise as a 'Notary' in England, so that he could work with English people buying holiday homes and private villas in Spain.

It all sounded rather glamorous to Dawn, who imagined wealthy clients buying glittering white villas overlooking the impossibly blue Mediterranean sea, employing Orlando and his company to do the conveyancing.

Dawn had been to Benidorm. She knew what an exotic

and heady place Spain could be.

Quite apart from the fact that he was an absolute hunk, he obviously had a very bright future, she thought and was several notches above just those with 'A' levels and aspirations she had met at college so far. Yet he had not asked her out.

She had her phone number written on one of Oakshott, Parslow and Partners 'compliments slips' in her bag, ready to give him had he asked, but no business had resulted and she could not understand why.

'Men!' she exclaimed, and gave her college bag another kick.

-oOo-

Rosalind had always got on well with Helen when they worked together and they were close friends now.

Helen now worked in Waitrose, of course, and since Rosalind had been made redundant they obviously saw less of each other, but they were happy to be catching up now over a quick lunch in Miriam's Tea Rooms, by the recreation ground.

'I'm sure,' said Rosalind, 'that he wasn't listening to a word we said and it was only when Mr Brownlow, the manager, asked him to explain something that he woke up. Arrogant little pig, he was.'

'Well do you know who he is?' asked Helen, 'He's the only the son of Duncan Ellis, one of the partners of Stiffhams, who according to Mr Shotter is a horrible little half-pint-sized man who bullies his staff and sacks people on a daily basis.'

'That would explain it. Like father like son.' Rosalind nodded, taking another sip of her tea.

'I shouldn't want that little twerp dealing with anything as important as my mortgage,' Helen said, 'Not that I could afford one anyway. I'd look elsewhere if I were you, Rosalind.'

'Still no chance of Paul making an honest woman of you and showering you with diamonds then?'

'No,' said Helen, pushing her teacup aside, 'He says we need to save up more first, so we can afford to get married.'

'Wasn't he saying that two years ago?' Rosalind looked at her friend with concern while dabbing the corners of her mouth with her paper napkin.

'Three years, more like. Still, I'm saving more since I started at Waitrose; the staff discount scheme is great and I save loads on food shopping.'

'Still no vacancies there, I suppose,' asked Rosalind.

'Sorry. But I'll tell you as soon as anything comes up, of course.'

'Thanks, Helen.'

'Well, I'd better be getting back or the vacancy coming up will be my job. Lovely to see you Rosalind, we must do it more often.'

The two young women embraced and Rosalind walked slowly back to the flat. She, at least, was not in a hurry to be anywhere and she used the time to think about the house and what she would do to it if they were lucky enough to actually get it.

-oOo-

The weekend passed in a sort of blur.

Geoff had the strange task of showing some prospective buyers around 2 Easton Drive, the house that not so very long ago he himself had viewed and, on that fateful day, his life had completely turned upside down.

The lawyers took their time, of course; it was how they justified their fees, and the divorce proceedings hadn't really got underway yet but at least his wife, shortly to be his former wife, had been very decent about it.
She agreed they hadn't really anything in common anymore and said that while she was surprised that he had been the one to find somebody else, she didn't hate him for it and so long as the financial arrangements could be 'fair and equitable' she was happy enough that they would part.

It was a pity that Janet was selling 2 Easton Drive, though. He thought it was a lovely house and had always liked the estate it was on, but she had explained that she had some family business to take care of and needed to put some money into that.

It was not in Geoff's nature to pry, and it was Janet's house after all, but he did wonder what type of family business could occasion the sale of a house that Janet said she grew up in and was very fond of.
Be that as it may, Geoff had decided that if Janet wanted to tell him anything about it then she would. He had said that if ever she needed any help or wanted to discuss it, he would always be ready to do what he could.

Janet explained that she had a notion to buy a little cottage nearer the town where her friend Lucy lived. When she also said that 2 Easton Drive was too big really for just a couple like them anyway, he had rejoiced that she had included him in her plans.

He didn't really care where he lived so long as it was with Janet, and when she asked if he would take her round the estate agents to start looking for their new home together, he was overjoyed.

-oOo-

Chapter 6

As she thought now about their lives together, Pauline knew that Barry had come along just at the right moment in her life.

He was very clever with finance and insurance and all that sort of thing and when her mother died and the house became hers, he arranged for her to take out a small mortgage on it which she used to buy a brand new car to replace her wheezing old Peugeot. That car had spent more time in the menders' than it did on the road.

She knew that you shouldn't really use mortgages to buy cars, but Barry showed her how much cheaper the repayments were than a car loan from the bank and that made the difference between yet another second-hand car and a brand new Volkswagen Golf. There was even some extra which paid for new carpets in the hall stairs and landing. The rest of it Barry arranged to invest in a Trust Fund through his firm, which would hold their savings and included a bit of life insurance to pay out if one of them died before the mortgage came to an end to pay it all off.

She ought to have a look through the papers and find the details of all that, she thought, given the limited time Barry had left. At least it might pay for the funeral costs, which if you believed the adverts on the telly, were likely to be horrendous.

It was a pity that her mother never really got the chance to get to know Barry, she thought. She might not have approved of his betting on horses and his drinking buddies, but she would have enjoyed the visits to stately homes, picnics in the country, walks on the beach and all that sort of thing that they did together. Pauline would miss that side of Barry very much when he was gone.

As the television in the corner blared out yet another advert for some funeral plan, Barry seemed to be waking up.

She was holding his hand, which gave an involuntary spasm as his eyes focused on her.

'Hello, Janet,' he said, and then closed his eyes again.

Well, he might have got her name wrong, and she didn't think she knew anyone called Janet, but at least Barry knew somebody was with him, thought Pauline.

-o0o-

Sylvia had been quite correct, of course. Bryn was after money.

He said he wanted an advance of two thousand pounds to put down as a deposit on a flat he had found to rent.

Sylvia couldn't resist asking if his new girlfriend was contributing anything to the deposit, and predictably Bryn blew his top.

Needless to say the conversation ended with her promising to transfer the money into his bank account, and they left it at that.

Throughout their turbulent marriage, Sylvia had always been in charge of the money. In the early days Bryn would turn on his puppy-dog eyes and simper that he wanted her to give him some pocket money because he had been a good boy. But later, as their relationship got more disfunctional, he would say she should spank him if he hadn't been good, but please could he have the pocket money anyway.

Sylvia was usually revolted by Bryn's perverted ideas of bedroom fun and Bryn rarely got his way there, but where money was concerned, although Sylvia controlled the purse strings, he usually got what he wanted one way or another.

Take the example of the ludicrous sports car.

Bryn had twittered on about it each time they walked past the showroom and was becoming a bore about it when they were at home too, until Sylvia finally lost patience and put her foot down. They had a perfectly good car which was not very old, she said, and they certainly didn't need one with only two doors and a sort of umbrella for a roof, which probably drank petrol and would cost a fortune to run.

That was on the Monday. On the Friday Bryn turned up in the wretched thing.
He had taken out a 'pay-day loan' at ruinous interest rates and bought it behind her back.

To sort it out Sylvia had had to arrange to pay off the loan before it bankrupted them, including paying the 'early repayment penalty', which really hurt.
The car itself was a heap of trouble and was falling apart. Three months later (because, of course, Bryn had not thought to insist on the dealer providing any sort of warranty to pay for the repairs), it went off to one of those companies that claim they will buy your car and then chisel the price down when you try to complete the deal.

They lost a lot of money on that little bit of nonsense, but it was typical of Bryn's irresponsible attitude, and even then he didn't seem to learn. Putting Sylvia firmly in charge of the finances was only sensible and although he didn't like it, Bryn still had to live with the consequences now.

-oOo-

Martin listened and did his best to concentrate as Mr Brownlow explained what the procedure was at the meeting he had had to miss with Jonathan, the in-house mortgage broker.

Most of it was about establishing the applicant's identity officially, and stuff to do with money laundering. Martin was surprised that selling houses involved quite so much paperwork, but did his best to follow it all.

From Stiffhams' point of view, Mr Brownlow continued, the principal point of the meeting with the applicants was to sell them insurance which related to their mortgage. That made some sense to Martin, but then it seemed the idea was to find out how much 'disposable income' the applicants had left over once the mortgage and household expenses were paid each month and to introduce other insurance products to sell them to soak some of it up.

They covered the obvious, such as buildings and contents insurance and life insurance to pay the mortgage off if they died before paying it all back, but then there was health insurance, insurance to cover redundancy, investment planning, and even insurance to cover any pets they might have. All these things carried commission for the estate agency business as a whole, but not necessarily for the employees responsible for selling the house, so Martin could perhaps be forgiven for letting his attention wander as Mr Brownlow's lengthy explanations went on.

He glanced through the window, between the plastic photograph hangers and noticed, to his surprise,

Dawn DeSantos coming towards the office.

He knew Dawn had a job at Oakshott, Parslow & Partners, the solicitors just over the road, of course, but he did not expect her to visit the estate agent's office. Presumably, he thought, it would take her some time to be able to save up enough to buy a house on trainee lawyer's wages.

Martin had been one of a group of boys at school who regarded Dawn as lovely to look at certainly, but somewhat aloof. She had always had older boyfriends from outside school and seemed to move in circles which did not involve her school peers, even in the sixth form.

Secretly, of course, Martin fancied Dawn like crazy. She was an early adopter of more adult clothes and, as soon as they got to the sixth form and didn't have to wear school uniform any more, she looked fantastic. She never seemed to wear the same outfit twice and seemed to get sexier and sexier as each day went by.

Martin noticed that she had an envelope in her hand and as she approached the office door Steve was on his feet and opening it for her.

'Hello,' she said huskily, 'I have a letter for a Mr Brownlow ... oh, hello, Martin,' she added.

Mr Brownlow accepted the letter and said, 'Ah from Oakshott Parslow & Partners, I see. Thank you very much, Miss…?'

'DeSantos,' Dawn breathed, 'Dawn DeSantos,' and

turning on her trim heel she was gone.

'Well, well, well, Martin!' leered Steve as he watched her shapely back disappearing over the road, 'You kept her quiet, young man!'

Martin, now blushing hotly, began to babble out some reply when Mr Brownlow gave one of his little coughs and, as usual, all conversation stopped.

'Perhaps, Martin, you would be kind enough to make us all some tea now,' he said, and Martin needing no further excuse to remove himself, scuttled into the back room to boil the kettle.

-oOo-

As usual, Geoff opened the car door for Janet. They were both looking forward to this little trip.

Janet had looked up details and made a shortlist of properties she thought they might like to view and, with Geoff acting as chauffeur, they had a route all worked out.

'First of all we have to call at the other branch of Stiffhams,' Janet was saying now, 'That nice Mr Brownlow at the local one has arranged for someone there to print off some details for us of one or two of the houses that we will view outside.'

They had been over this several times already and Geoff thought Janet's excited chatter was charming.

'I've never actually bought a house before,' she had

explained last night, 'having inherited this one, I mean, so I'm not quite sure of the procedure.'

Geoff felt very protective as he explained that the process only got painful later on, when the lawyers got involved, but that the first bit involving viewing the houses, could actually be quite fun.

'Thank goodness I've got you to help me, Geoff,' she said, 'And it will be as much your choice of house as mine, you know. It will be our home together.'

If Geoff could have had that last sentence engraved on his heart he could not have been happier.
At the time he had said something stupid like 'It is very kind of you, Janet.' and with a laugh she replied that she couldn't leave him to sleep in the street, could she.

Later that night, as they got into bed, Geoff had his thoughts in a better order and said
'I can think of nothing that will make me happier than sharing a home with you, Janet, but you must let me pay half the cost, you know.'

The room was only illuminated by Janet's dazzling mischievous smile as she turned out the light and said 'Half the cost? I thought you were buying me a house so I could be your kept woman!'

Geoff chucked as he drew her close and said,
'Come here, then. It's time to practise paying the rent!'

-oOo-

Chapter 7

Mary Maloney lived in a small village on the outskirts of Dublin until, three days after her fifteenth birthday, she was bundled into a taxi and driven to a forbidding-looking Victorian edifice in the city where she was sedated until her labour was over.

She was told, none too kindly, that her baby was dead and as she left, the bristling nun who showed her to the door, told her she was a cheap little tart who deserved to live a life of penance until she died and went to burn for all eternity in the fires of Hell.

She never went back to the village or the church where the priest had had his way with her and after a brief stay in a boarding house, her father, who had secured work in the Liverpool docks moved the whole family to England, and the matter was never spoken of again.

-o0o-

Barry Patrick knew that his mother's name might have been Maloney, but then again it could have been O'Leary, Smith or any one of a handful of names of women and girls who had their babies taken for adoption in Dublin on the day he was born.

All Barry really knew for certain was his birthday and that he was born in Dublin. His adoptive parents lived in North London and although he asked them, they never revealed anything about his birth parents. But then, he supposed, they may not have known anything beyond the fact that he came from an orphanage in Dublin where they originally lived and where they married.

His adoptive father took a job as a postman in London before Barry's first birthday and they lived a chaotic life moving from one rented house to another, trying to keep one step ahead of the bailiffs as he grew up.

At sixteen he joined the Royal Navy and then two years later, secured a job as a 'junior' in an office within walking distance of the foster care centre which had housed him when his adoptive parents split up.

In the early days, when he started with the insurance company, Barry was sent to work in a department that matched the details of life insurance claims to the policy history, to make sure premiums had been paid and ensure that the company was liable to pay out when the death of the policyholder was reported to them.

Initially, Barry had to manually file certified copies of Death Certificates. A few months later he was trusted to log the names and details of new claimants onto an ancient and temperamental computer system. It was quite exacting and detailed work and he showed some aptitude for it which won him friends in the office, who would rather spend their time on less menial tasks.

His efforts gave Barry information about who had died, when and where, and access to some of their family background through Census information. When deaths were reported where the place of birth was Dublin, Barry often wondered if his own real family still lived there, and on one day the accidental death was reported of a young man with the same birthday as his own who was born in an orphanage in Dublin, and according to the records, then adopted.

Barry was captivated by the tragic story. Could this be the same orphanage where he was born?

For several months he could find nothing much more about the orphanage except that it had been run by the Catholic Church and was closed down some years earlier when some sort of underhand practice there was exposed in the Press.

Barry found out that some records had survived and that it was possible for 'responsible registered organisations' to research details of those born there. A 'responsible registered organisation' included insurance companies, he discovered, and he began to ask about as to how he could find out more.

It took him two years to get a short list of names of women who had given birth at the institution on his own birthday, and he chose Mary Maloney at random to see what he could find.

A Mary Eileen Maloney had produced a baby with the correct date of birth. She was born in Dublin and aged twenty-two, had married a John Raymond Bassett in England. They produced a daughter, named Janet Mary, having been married for eighteen months, according to Census records. Barry thought he was onto something.

It all came together for him when he discovered that his own insurance company had insured the life of John Raymond Bassett and paid out when he died in a motor accident.

That gave Barry an address and it was just a short step to establish, via Local Authority records that Mary Eileen Bassett (Nee Maloney) and her daughter Janet Mary still lived at the same address.

It just might be, Barry thought, and even if it wasn't it could lead somewhere.

Barry had been promoted to the Life Insurance Division and, like everyone in that department, had been given the ability to claim commission if he introduced people to the business who subsequently bought insurance products. It meant his access to the records he had been studying diminished but he was still based in the same building and already had much of the information he required.

He spent a few careful weeks checking his facts and

hatched a plan as to what he was going to do.

The little rented studio flat in London he called home was only a relatively short train ride from 2 Easton Drive, where Mary and Janet Bassett still lived, as far as he could establish.

-oOo-

It was all so terribly expensive, Mike thought as he shuffled the papers on his desk once more.

The mortgage he had expected, of course, but all these insurance things they seemed to need would put up the monthly outgoings much more than he had thought.

There was so much of it. There was even an insurance policy to cover children they might have in the future. Mike noticed a pained look in Rosalind's eyes when that flash little git of a mortgage broker started on about it.

Why did they need a 'plan', as he called it, to cover their school fees when they hadn't even got any kids and they would probably have to go to the local comprehensive school anyway?

Mike sighed. If all this meant Rosalind would be happy he would find a way to do it, of course and he wondered if he dare approach his boss and ask for a raise.

This lot was going to cost and the realisation as to quite how much, was beginning to make him nervous.

The breakthrough came when Rosalind recounted the details of her conversation over lunch with Helen.

She had explained who that frightful little mortgage broker actually was and suggested they look elsewhere.

Mike had sort of taken it as read that they were going to use the agent's in-house mortgage service and the agents seemed to assume that they would too. But why should they?

There was nothing to say they had to, so Mike had a look on the internet and found an absolute torrent of information about independent mortgage brokers who would be willing to help them. Some didn't even want a fee, but Rosalind made a call to Helen, who pointed out that someone had to pay them, so they would be getting commission from the mortgage providers or insurance companies involved. That might mean they only offered the products that gave them the best commission, rather than what was best for Mike and Rosalind.

In the end they called a company who were very up-front about their fees, set out just this conflict of interest in their blurb, and explained that they would not even discuss insurance until a suitable mortgage had been found, and only then if their clients wanted their advice.

To Mike's astonishment, the three best mortgage choices they came up with were all cheaper than the one Jonathan Ellis, the agent's man, was pushing and were from High Street names they had heard of.

The difference in cost more than covered the broker's fee and the ease with which the whole thing could be set up, with the added confidence that this broker was on their side and working only for them, made Mike and Rosalind bold.

With an 'in principle' agreement with one of the largest Building Societies in place twenty-four hours later, Mike and Rosalind made an offer for the house, which was immediately accepted, and they were on their way to buying their first home.

-oOo-

Pauline was unsure what to do but the vicar and the nurse were quite clear. She simply had to report it to the police.

Barry had difficulty with speech, but on occasions, if he took his time, he could string coherent sentences together. She was not expecting the little speech he had just made, however, and it shocked her to the core.

'Hello Pauline, love,' he had said, 'I can't hide it from you any longer, I've got to tell you. I'm very sorry but I made your mother fall down the stairs on purpose. I didn't push her, I just scared her at the top so she fell.'

On that awful day all those years ago when she came home from work and found her mother's body in a pool of blood at the bottom of the stairs, Barry was at the races. He didn't get back until quite late and had obviously had a bit to drink.

He was up and dressed and as far as she knew about to go out of the door as she left for work that morning, but now it seemed he waited and caused her mother's accident. Or did he?

Was it an accident? It was quite hard to understand what Barry was saying and when that nice policewoman came, it took nearly an hour to get him to repeat what he had told her. But everyone felt Pauline had to report what he said. He seemed, after all to be claiming responsibility for her mother's death, if not actually her murder.

The policewoman asked him why he did it and without any hesitation he said,
'So Pauline would inherit the house, of course. She needed the money for a new car, you see.'

Murder? The word horrified Pauline. The Coroner had stated that it was highly likely that her mother had fallen to her death, there was no sign of a struggle or any wounds that could be attributed to an attack. Could you murder someone by scaring them so they fell down the stairs?
According to the detective who arrived a little later, you could, if it was premeditated.

Barry should have been at the races with his friend, Tiny. Perhaps Tiny would remember if he was there.

Of course he would! Silly of her! This was just Barry's dementia talking. If the police talked to Tiny it would clear the matter up in a minute!

Pauline told them where Tiny worked and started to relax. She felt rather foolish for setting this hare running and decided she must apologise to the nice policewoman when she saw her again, if she ever did, for being so silly.

-oOo-

To Barry, in his lucid moments, an image of the bedroom door stood out in the sharpest focus in his thoughts.

He was back in that morning when he had stood behind that bedroom door listening.

There was no question that having the bathroom downstairs was an inconvenience … Ha! 'an inconvenience'! Barry chuckled at his own little joke. Having to go down the steep narrow stairs in the little Victorian house when half asleep demanded concentration. He himself had slipped more than once on the threadbare carpet while negotiating this journey. It was particularly unpleasant on a cold and frosty morning when, if barefoot, the ancient cold decorative tiles in the hallway below offered no welcome to the intrepid traveller. Barry had learned his lesson soon after moving in with Pauline, and bought himself some slippers.

It would be all too easy to fall and Barry planned just such a fall now.

Pauline's mother was already frail and one of those women who insisted on wearing shawls and sandals with the buckles undone. This flappy clothing and loose footwear choice was asking for trouble in a Victorian house with thin carpets, steep stairs and Barry lurking behind bedroom doors.

At last, as Barry replayed the scene in his mind, she emerged from her own bedroom, clutching her stick in one hand and an empty teacup and saucer in the other.

Pauline always took her mother tea before she left for work in the morning and her mother would manoeuvre down the stairs each day on her way to the bathroom with her stick and cup and saucer in opposite hands. That left nothing with which to hold the admittedly slim and quite inadequate rail as she descended. Barry had watched her do this several times.

With his own door open just a crack he could see when she shambled her way to the top of the stairs.

'Boo!' said Barry, yanking open the door and waving his arms about.

His mother-in-law gasped, stumbled and fell. That was all it took.

He left it a few minutes before he went to check,

although if the loud slap and crack of bones was anything to go by as she reached the end of her journey, Barry was pretty confident that gravity and the hard tiles in the hall had done their work and he would not have to intervene to finish the job.

When, having combed his hair, straightened his tie and adjusted his belt, Barry eventually went down the stairs himself, he was confident that a corpse awaited him on the decorative tiled door at the bottom and a quick check for a pulse confirmed his diagnosis.

He stepped over the body, carefully avoiding the pool of blood by the head and set off, as planned, for Sandown Park and a day at the races.

-oOo-

Chapter 8

Sylvia sent an excited email to Bryn who replied immediately to the effect that the offer for the house was fine by him and asked when he could have his money.

Of course there was much to do before that question could be answered, but it was with an uplifted heart that Sylvia visited the offices of Oakshott, Parslow & Partners, and asked to see Mrs Pauline Patrick who was handling the matter of the sale of her house.

She was somewhat taken aback to find that Mrs Patrick was not in the office and she realised she should have thought to phone first, but the girl who came down to Reception to explain seemed quite upset.

That girl was Dawn DeSantos of course, who earlier that morning had been told by the Senior Partner, no less, that Pauline's husband had died during the night and they should not expect her in for a while.

Dawn had to explain to callers, including Sylvia, that a temporary cover, or locum solicitor, would be appointed in the next day or so and that business would continue uninterrupted, once he or she was in post.

She practised the lines she was expected to say to her reflection in the grubby window of Pauline's office, but this news had come as a shock to Dawn, and now on her own in the Conveyancing Department, she felt very exposed and uncertain.
As a result when Sylvia arrived she gabbled out the words and had to stop half way through to choke back tears.

Fortunately Dawn knew Sylvia, or Miss Pendle as she had been called when she worked at her school, and it was not long before Miss Pendle was comforting her and lending her a grey handkerchief to dry her eyes.

Dawn was embarrassed, flushed and flustered, and when the fat receptionist waddled over to see what the matter was, she was ashamed that she had not shown herself at her best and behaved more like an adult.

-oOo-

'So let me be sure I've got this clear,' said Detective Sergeant Morris, 'You met Barry Patrick at Sandown Park racecourse as agreed and gave him the betting slip?'

'Yes,' Ivor 'Tiny' Washington replied, 'Barry knew he was going to be late so he asked me to meet him on the course and put some money on Serenity Maid in the first race, so he didn't miss the chance to back her.'

'And the horse won?'

'Yes, and at excellent odds, so Barry did rather well on that. We both did.'

So the betting slip gave Barry a timed alibi to prove that he was at Sandown Park rather than at home, D.S. Morris thought. Very clever.

Although the betting slip was never actually needed to support his alibi as it turned out, it provided Barry with an insurance policy which, given his profession at the time, was typical of the man.

'Look, I'm sorry officer, but what has this all got to do with the Janet Bassett letter?' Tiny Washington asked now.

'Ah,' said the Detective Sergeant, maintaining his placid appearance, 'I will be coming to that. Are you aware that Mrs Pauline Patrick's mother died on the same day that you had arranged to meet Barry Patrick at Sandown Park?'

'I'm sorry officer, I don't think I follow ...'

'Allow me to explain then. Barry Patrick, as you may know, has dementia, so we must be careful how much credence we give to anything he may say, but when his wife visited he became agitated and started talking about Mrs Patrick's late mother and stated that he did not push her down the stairs. Perhaps I should mention that she was found at the bottom of the stairs having apparently fallen to her death. Mr Patrick has told Mrs Patrick that he watched her fall and when he established that she was in fact dead, he stepped over the body and left the house to join you, cool as a cucumber, at the races. The matter was referred to the police, which is why we are discussing it today.'

-oOo-

In anticipation of an early move, Sylvia started clearing things up.

She had done the airing cupboard and, rather than tackle the shed as it was looking like rain, she just got the ladder out and went for a look in the loft.

As far as she knew there was only the perennial plastic Christmas tree and a forlorn box of decorations up there that Bryn brought out each year. Not last year though, that was a grim Christmas when shiny baubles and tinsel would have added nothing festive to the chilly atmosphere.

Sylvia slid the loft hatch aside and groped about for the light switch, thinking she hadn't actually been up here herself since they moved in, as far as she could recall.

With the light on, she scrambled up the last steps of the ladder and wriggled into the unfamiliar space.

There was the little Christmas tree, carefully wrapped

in dustbin sacks to keep the dust off, and the box of decorations.
But there was something else.

As her eyes got used to the gloomy light she saw two more large cardboard boxes and leaning on the chimney breast, some forgotten, unfinished paintings.

Bryn must have put them up here when he seemed to go off painting a year or so ago.

Carefully, so as not to crack her head on the various beams or step off the small area with a chipboard floor, Sylvia approached the little stash.

One of the two boxes once contained wine, according to the label on the side, and Sylvia recognised it as the repository for Bryn's artist's materials. The other larger box was wrapped in a dustbin sack and she undid the loose knot at the top to see what it contained.

As the contents were revealed she recoiled and, straightening up rapidly, banged her head on an unseen beam. What met her gaze, in two piles, was a stack of 'girlie magazines' and a separate pile of much harder pornographic ones.
The second collection had pictures of men doing things to men, girls in handcuffs or chained to strong machinery, men in masks holding whips and chains and all sorts of other revolting activities.

Once more, Bryn's tastes disgusted her. She had no

idea he had such material and wondered if he had forgotten it when he moved out.

Next she looked at the canvases leaning against the chimney breast.

The first two were unfinished work and it was difficult to see what they were depicting. Next there were two new blank canvases and then Sylvia's fingers fell on another slightly smaller but dreadfully shocking picture.

In Bryn's almost cartoonish impressionistic style this one was a portrait of a muscle-bound naked man reclining with one large foot up on the frame of a candy striped deckchair.
Bryn had given his model a tiny pin-head with just one leering eye and ridiculously enlarged genitalia which came over the edge of the seat and almost reached the floor by his other foot.

This hideous painting almost caused Sylvia to bang her head again on the low beams, but she steadied herself and decided what to do.

Tomorrow she would go to the hardware store and buy one of those incinerators that look like an old fashioned dustbin with a chimney on the top of the lid. She would not tell Bryn about her discovery or ask him what he wanted done with it.
She would have another of her little bonfires and burn the lot of it, hopefully out of sight of the neighbours.

Bryn, she told herself, was a depraved, sex-mad creep

and she was going to burn him out of her life if it took all day.

-oOo-

Pauline had expected it, of course, but when it actually happened it still came as a shock.

But Barry's death was not half as much of as blow as what happened two days afterwards, when all these policemen arrived and started talking about fraud and impersonation and all sorts.

That nice policewoman had been there fortunately, and had done a sterling job of making all these people tea and even making Pauline a sandwich when she realised she had forgotten to have lunch or breakfast that day.

It was a good job she was there because what that Detective Sergeant had to say was nasty, very nasty indeed.

Was Barry a conman? And what was all this about his sister?

Pauline knew he didn't have a sister or any family at all and was adopted from birth, but now the detective said two-thirds of Barry's nursing home fees were paid by his sister.
There was obviously some mistake, she had said, but the detective explained he had confirmation from Barry's friend from work, Tiny Washington, who she knew was some sort of specialist insurance lawyer.

Alone now, for what seemed the first time in ages, Pauline sat on the edge of her chair and stared blankly into space. Her life was unraveling around her and she felt powerless to deal with it. She didn't like it one bit.

-o0o-

Sylvia's new incinerator worked a treat.

Admittedly initially it smelled awful as whatever it was they put on the raw metal to stop it rusting burned off, but after that it quickly and effectively created a fiery grave for the repulsive paintings and even the unused canvases she found in the loft.

Next she hauled down the heavy box with the pornographic magazines, and setting it beside the dustbin like incinerator, fed them into the flames.

At first, once she realised she had to tear the pages out to get them to light, the metal chimney on the top produced a little flame but mercifully very little smoke. Every now and than Sylvia fed a broom handle through the handle to lift the lid and add more fuel to the fire.

As she gained confidence, she also came to realise quite how many magazines there were to burn, and she started adding the pages fifteen or twenty at a time. When this stifled the flames and threatened to put the blaze out she began to tear the pages from the magazines at the rate of eight or nine at a time, and adding them every couple of minutes.

Unfortunately this slower pace gave Sylvia time to notice the gross images she was committing to the flames and it would not be going to far to say she was horrified.

What anyone could find enjoyable or even mildly titillating in such material was completely beyond her, and as much as she could, she increased the speed she was adding the revolting pages to the fire.

When her phone rang she was momentarily distracted as she struggled to get it out of her pocket and answer the call.

It was just another of those recorded scam calls and she quickly shut it off, but not before two or three almost intact pages, rising on the heat, escaped through the little chimney and floated high in the air, heading in the direction of the vicar's much prized rose garden, next door but one.

-oOo-

Chapter 9

'I suppose this is about Janet Bassett this time,' said Ivor 'Tiny' Washington.

At the start of their earlier interview, before Barry died, DS Morris had explained that he wanted to talk to him about the death of Barry's mother-in-law and something he had said about it.

DS Morris had not yet mentioned any names but he was long enough in the job to know that correcting a witness who might have something interesting to tell without prompting was unwise.

'Perhaps you could tell us about Janet Bassett, Mr Washington,' he said now.

'Well, I mean, it was Barry's idea of course. He thought if he could demonstrate that he was her brother he could get her to set up that Trust Fund for them both. The rather sweet idea being it would protect them both, so they could pay into it to cover each other if anything happened to either of them. But you probably know all that. My only involvement was to provide the letter, on Stokes and Potts headed paper, to confirm that they were related.'

'Go on,' said DS Morris, intrigued.

'Yes, well, I know it was wrong and I realise I am for it now, but you see I owed quite a bit of money to some rather impatient bookmakers and he offered to clear my debts if I did this letter for him. At the time it seemed harmless enough. I mean to say, Barry had done all the necessary research and was completely convinced she was his sister and he felt he needed to protect her as well as himself. Rather a demonstration of his generous nature, I felt.'

'Thank you, Mr Washington. For the record could you just explain your relationship with Stokes and Potts.'

DS Morris had no idea where all this was leading and it had nothing at all to do with why he had wanted to speak to Ivor 'Tiny' Washington, but his professional interest had been aroused and he wanted to get o the bottom of this story.

'I'd only just decided to leave, you see. Barry said he was pretty sure he could get me a job here and, well it seemed a chance to … to move things on. So I got some of their notepaper and typed up the letter.'

'How did you get the notepaper?' DS Morris asked now.

'Well that was easy. The office I worked in was right by the reception and the typist who sat in there had the letterheads in a desk drawer. When she went out to lunch I just helped myself.'

There was a knock at the door and a uniformed police officer stood on the other side of the glass panel.

'Excuse me for one moment, Mr Washington,' said DS Morris, and went to see the officer.

'Sorry to disturb you, sir,' he said, 'I've got Washington's employment records as you requested and I thought you might want them straight away.'

DS Morris flicked through the thin file. Sure enough, Ivor 'Tiny' Washington had taken up his present post with the insurance company after leaving Stokes and Potts, Solicitors, in Wales.

'Thank you, officer. Can you run a check on a Janet Bassett for me, please. Might be a relative of Barry Patrick.

-oOo-

As Clive found a seat and settled down with his customary Scotch and American, on the 17:21 out of Waterloo, he took a moment to reflect on what an extraordinary day it had been.

When he arrived for work, eleven minutes late after a delay outside Wimbledon, the place was crawling with police. And then, by lunchtime, the word got round that Tiny Washington from the Legal Section had been arrested and carted off.

Plain-clothes police were much in evidence in the afternoon, looking through files in Clive's own department and two of them had obviously been granted access to the computer system as they were beavering away on one of the terminals and printing off documents, while another one stood by the printer to collect up what came out.

All very mysterious.

The rumour mill was having a field day, of course and it wasn't long before theories ranging from theft to international money laundering were filling up everyones' internal inboxes.
By the time the train reached Clapham Common, Clive was pretty sure which of the potential causes for what was obviously a raid, he preferred.

The attention seemed to move from old Tiny's department to his own and several people were taken off to meeting rooms for discussions with the police. But Clive had noticed a trend.

Those interviewed were mostly the chaps who went to the races together at the weekend, and perhaps more importantly were all members of the little group of sportsmen who studied the form together over the Sporting Life each morning.

Clive had been one of their number himself until, a couple of years ago, an unwise investment in a 'dead cert, that couldn't lose if it tried' came in well down the running order at Haydock Park, and having lost a packet on the beast he had to own up and then promise his wife never to try picking winners again, on pain of being locked out of the marital home.

The link slowly forming in Clive's mind between old Tiny and the sportsmen might be Barry Patrick, he thought. Barry was big pals with Tiny before his stroke and they used to spend time together at Barry's London flat during the working week.

Tiny was not lucky with the horses, and being only a junior-ish in-house solicitor, was not terribly flush most of the time. As far as Clive knew, Tiny was a bachelor who lived out Surbiton way. With a penchant for betting and no guiding female to stay his hand, he suspected he had run up some gambling debts that perhaps he couldn't handle. Though what that had to do with the company, he couldn't say.

No doubt more would be revealed on Monday, he thought, and settled back in his seat. Thank goodness he had given up punting on the gee-gees when he did. Helga, his wife, may be a little direct in her speech at times and certainly made her opinion about gambling clear after that awful mistake at Haydock Park, but she was a wonderful woman who had saved him before from making a mess of his life.

She had saved his teeth too, he thought, and licked round the gleaming crowns she had installed in her professional life as his dentist. It couldn't be that often that love began in the dentist's chair.

-oOo-

Love for Ivor 'Tiny' Washington had been harder to

come by.

His sporting prowess at his school and his time in the front row for the London Welsh rugby team had given him a hard muscular body and keeping a magnificent physique was easy for him, but his shyness and fear of rejection made him an unlucky lover.

He loved one from a distance however, but could never speak his love because the object of his devotion was as red-blooded a heterosexual as you were likely to meet, so he contented himself with friendship and left it at that.

There had been lovers, of course. Back in Wales, at art college evening classes he had posed for a painter and they had seen quite a bit of each other. But that fell apart when the artist revealed his portrait.

It was a terrible impressionistic thing of him naked in a striped deckchair, although he had posed fully dressed. In the picture he had a pin head with one leering eye, a lolling tongue and enormous genitals hanging off the edge of the chair and almost reaching the ground.
He was horrified and made the artist promise to paint over it. He would have insisted on its destruction had not the painter pleaded with him that he could not afford to waste canvasses, and given their previous relationship he relented, but it left a bitter taste and they did not see each other again.

Tiny's own efforts with paint and easel were not

bad and although his grumpy tutor could only bring himself to describe his output as 'workmanlike' he tried hard with portraits of horses. They were horses' heads mostly, which were often admired when he had the courage to bring them out and put them on display.

His friendship with Barry Patrick had started with horses and horse racing and together they had visited racecourses all over the country. He was a regular visitor to Barry's little apartment over the garages round the back of Holborn and often stayed the weekend.

Their relationship was entirely platonic however, and while Tiny might have longed for more in the early days, his friendship with Barry was too precious to risk bringing any other elements into play.

After school Tiny joined Stokes and Potts, Solicitors, and worked his way laboriously through his legal studies to become qualified. He hated the work they gave him in the conveyancing department however, and when Barry got him the job in the in-house legal department at the insurance company, he was delighted to make the change and move to London.

Although his progress as a newly qualified lawyer was slow and he found promotion very hard to come by, the change did put him in closer contact with Barry, and for Tiny that was enough.

With Barry around Tiny had no time to be lonely.

Barry was larger than life and twice as much fun and if it wasn't for a little wrinkle in their financial dealings years ago, Tiny would have been very happy.

It was that little wrinkle, which he thought had been ironed out of history years ago, that the policeman wanted to talk to him about now and he was surprised at how much they had uncovered.

-oOo-

Chapter 10

Rosalind reached for her phone, but before she could scroll to Mike's number she had to rush to the toilet.

There she was comprehensively, spectacularly and joyfully sick.

She had never been so happy in her life.

Earlier she had been to the chemist to replace the tests which had, after all, been in the cupboard for months, so might have been inaccurate, she reasoned. But the new tests confirmed it. Rosalind was pregnant at last.

-oOo-

Orlando parked his Porsche at the edge of the car park, just beyond the newly resurfaced section. He did not want tar stains on his clothes.

He stepped athletically from the low vehicle and looked around him.

The Victorian building he faced was clearly built as a shop with, he thought, the upper parts originally being the living accommodation of the proprietors. Now, however, it served in its entirety as offices.

It was, he noticed, a little grimy and in need of a fresh coat of paint here and there, but, as he smoothed the impeccable ceases in his expensive suit trousers and lifted the little brown leather briefcase from the seat, he smiled to himself. Working, albeit briefly, for Oakshott, Parslow and Partners, would give him a very useful insight into the workings of what he assumed was a typical busy conveyancing department in a provincial English solicitor's office. The experience he would gain would help him to advise his father how their new London office should be set up when they were ready to open it.

-oOo-

The call to the college at first met with confusion.

Normally, in these circumstances one of the lecturers would be able to cover local solicitor's offices in the event of an unforeseen absence; and the local lawyers all looked to the college to help them out if this sort of situation arose. But this was the start of the holiday season and many of the staff had taken a few early days off to avoid the annual package-tour price-hike as the school holidays started, and the college had nobody to spare.

Fortunately the emergency only involved

'conveyancing' so they were not being asked to provide specialist lawyers or anyone particularly highly qualified, but the only person in the entire college with even enough qualifications to handle that lowly position was one of the 'mature students' who, whilst able to practise in his own right, was with them now for a short course to study the process of becoming a 'Notary'; and he was Spanish.

The department heads were delighted to learn that he spoke flawless English, understood conveyancing in England and was willing to help out. Fortunately his qualifications exceeded those usually needed to conduct basic domestic house sales and purchases in England by some margin.

This amiable Spanish fellow also said he would relish the chance to work in a provincial solicitor's conveyancing office to gain the experience, so the Head of Department told the Senior Partner of Oakshott, Parslow and Partners, that if this Spanish chap's work could be signed off and underwritten by one of their Partners, he was sure Orlando would fit the bill for the few days of cover that was needed.

Orlando watched as the chubby receptionist made her ponderous way to the kettle in the back kitchen to prepare his coffee. We will be needing a proper coffee machine in London, he noted.

-oOo-

Glancing at his phone as it rang, Geoff was pleased to see that the caller was Roberta 'Bobbie' Bassington.

This delightful if rather high-spirited girl was the daughter of his ex-wife's sister, who lived with her mother in the moth-eaten, but once rather grand, family home in Barton Matravers, Wilts.

Geoff had always liked Roberta and fortunately his affection was returned. This was just as well for she was a girl of strong passions who, when roused, was quite likely to start something.

With her petite frame, vivid auburn hair, pert upturned nose and large green eyes she was certainly very attractive, but those eyes could also shoot flames for up to ten feet if she was thwarted in any of her little plans or schemes, as several of her short-lived boyfriends had found to their cost.

Most of the time, however, Roberta was full of fun and a delightful charming girl. At least that was the general view of most of the cloud of hapless lovelorn suiters who followed her around.

These estimable features, apart perhaps from the flame-shooting eyes, were not in evidence however when Geoff answered the call.

'Why, Uncle Geoffrey dear, has your wife inflicted her foul company on the old family home with, it would seem, the intention of making an extended stay?' she said.

'Eh?' said Geoff, not abreast.

'This loathsome aunt seems to have dug herself into the woodwork and refuses even the strongest entreaties to be gone. Have you been being unkind to her? And what suggestion have you for removing this impossible-to-satisfy human complaints department from the once peaceful old home and rolling sunlit lawns of Matravers Hall?'

Roberta had recently graduated from Girton College, Cambridge and given her manner of speech Geoff wondered if she had been reading a little more Edwardian literature than was good for her.

'I'm sorry, I don't think I ...' he blustered.

'You heard, you old blister. Why is your estranged wife here when she has a perfectly good house on the outskirts of a very pleasant bit of suburban commuter belt to infest instead?'

'I have no idea,' said Geoff, collecting his wits, 'She made no mention of it to me. Is she being a nuisance?'

'I should say so! She is a pest and a pestilence and a porcine petulant problem.'

'Now, Bobbie,' chided Geoff gently, 'Would you say "porcine"? Is that any way to describe a loved relative?'

'Well, perhaps that was a bit strong, but she has certainly put on weight since I saw her last and gulps down her meals with an unbecoming gusto the like of which I have not encountered before in all my young life. I wouldn't mind that so much as Matravers Hall has always done its guests well and been generous with the grub as you know, but I have been turfed out of the blue room to accommodate her spreading bulk and she parks her beastly Citroen in front of my dear little sports car, making a quiet sneak to the local pub for a little peace and quiet jolly difficult without alerting mother!'

Geoff stifled a chortle as he imagined her pique at these little inconveniences.

'I mean to say, fair enough that mother wheels out the fatted calf for her sister, I suppose, but your erstwhile wife had eaten it all before the more permanent members of the household got a look in. And she is never, ever, satisfied.'

'How do you mean?' asked Geoff, who, as it happened, had a fair idea what she meant.

'My dear adopted uncle-by-marriage, even you cannot have failed to notice her wheedling way of wanting things her own way and involving everyone in getting what she wants.
Why this very morning, just after breakfast, mark you, she had us rearranging the furniture in the sitting area of the blue room suite because the sun glinted in the mirror and caught her eye as she was trying to read her book, stretched out on the sofa like a beached whale!'

'A beached whale?'

'Yes, a big-breakfasted, bloated bulbous balloon of a beached whale. I'd just watched her consume three sausages, two fried eggs and most of the remaining bacon, after which she finished all the tea in the pot. And this spectacle, I might add, I was forced to endure after something of a late night at Rosy Brice-Waterman's twenty-first birthday party.'

'My wife went to Rosy Brice-Waterman's twenty first birthday party?' asked Geoff incredulously.

'No, but I did, you silly old uncle, and the morning head it left me with is still rather troubling me.'

'No wonder you are in a bad mood,' Geoff offered.

'I'm incandescent, inconvenienced, and incredibly fed up, and what I want to know is what is to be done about it?!'

'Well, I don't know that I …'

'No, I suppose your sphere of influence with the lady in question is somewhat reduced following recent events. How is the sparkling dentist by the way?'

'Janet is very well, thank you. I hope you will get to meet her soon. I'm sure you two would get on famously.'

'Yes well, perhaps we would, but before I run the eye over your new lady-love we must cope with your recent cast-off. It seems mother and I are left to clear up your mess, and were it not for ties of blood, I'm convinced mother would have bopped her with a chair leg by now.'

'Is it really that bad?'

'It's worse! Look Uncle Geoffrey, couldn't I come and stay with you for a week or two until she blows over? It is awfully inconvenient being down in the country at the moment and mother won't let me go anywhere while your former wife is on the premises, insisting I have to be around to help all the time.'

'I thought you regarded Matravers Hall as an earthly paradise?'

'It is, or was until recently …'

'Well then?'

'Well, all right, yes. The thing is, Uncle Geoffrey, you know how close we have always been and how much I love your company …'

'Come to the point, Bobbie, what are you really after?' said Geoff a little impatiently.

'Why, you old sweetie-pie, you always could read me like a book! It's why I regard you with such respect and deep affection and always look upon you more as a trusted and much loved friend and mentor than just an uncle by marriage …'

'Bobbie!'

'Oh, all right. Look, the thing is some friends from Uni have clubbed together to hire a boat for ten days to potter about on the Thames and I have been invited to join the consortium to lend a bit of glamour to the proceedings. But I can't go if mother continues to insist on my baby-sitting your blasted ex-wife.'

'I thought it would be something like that. Why can't your mother look after her herself?'

'Ah, that's where the difficulty arises. You see, mother has a longstanding arrangement to go to some literary retreat thing in Wales and read the unsuspecting inmates chunks of her ghastly books, right when this rather jolly trip on the Thames is due to take place.'

'I see,' Geoff smiled to himself. Roberta's plans always had little complications like this and rarely gained her mother's unconditional approval.

'Of course it wouldn't matter at all if your wretched reject hadn't decided to impose herself on us. If I can't shift her I shan't be able to go, and all my hopes and dreams are rather dependent on going.'

'Oh yes? And does this fellow have a name?'

'Fellow? I don't follow you, Uncle Geoffrey.'

'Yes, you do, you little minx. The fellow you hope to go on the boat trip with.'

'Ah, well. there is, I admit, a certain romantic interest in this little tale. You see Rosy Brice-Waterman's brother is going along as it happens …'

'And it is he who invited you?'

'Gosh, Uncle, you are such a detective! As you so cleverly divined, it was he who invited me! However did you work that out?!'

'And by saying you are staying with Janet and I, you will placate your mother and make her think you are under my doting and ever watchful eye, I take it?'

'Something in that, yes.' Roberta paused for breath, 'But none of that works if we can't winkle your horrible ex out of the family home!'

Geoff sighed.

'Roberta, you can always be relied upon to shake Hell's very foundations with your plans and schemes, but I think involving me in your little deception is rather naughty …'

'You won't do it?'

'I didn't say …'

'Oh, Uncle Geoffrey, you always used to call me Bobbie when you loved me. Have you forgotten all the fun we had with me sitting on your knee at the piano as you taught me to play 'chopsticks'; or that time we went to the Ritz for tea to celebrate your retirement; or that day at the races when …'

'Yes, yes, Bobbie. I know. But you ask a lot of me and

I confess I have no plan to get my wife to leave your house yet …'

'Not yet, perhaps, but you know how clever you are, dear Uncle Geoffrey … or should I call you Uncle Geoff now, like Janet does … I'm so looking forward to meeting her, by the way. And I'm so glad you have found happiness and can be with the one you love, while I, trapped in this crumbling old pile, surrounded, not by my lively and attractive peers, but forced to waste my young life with unrelenting drudgery at the hands of the older generations of our family …'

'Bobbie, please stop! I'm trying to think …'

'You are? You mean you might help after all? I knew I could rely on you, I can't imagine why I thought for a moment that you wouldn't be the knight in shining armour I have always seen you as, riding fearlessly to my rescue in your shining Jaguar … the same Jaguar that took us all on those lovely sun-drenched picnics, do you remember …'

'I'll hang up if you don't shut up, Bobbie! Now listen,' said Geoff, 'I might have an idea.'

-oOo-

Every other year, Janet explained, she had to attend a meeting with some family trustees or something, and Geoff had to fend for himself for the evening.

He had decided to get a Chinese meal delivered, and lacking the imagination to compose a menu of his own from the extensive list of dishes available, he ordered 'E for one' and waited, with the volume of the TV turned down so he did not miss the doorbell, and with sufficient plates, cutlery, bowls and paper napkins ready to deal with the feast when it arrived.

Janet set off with a fat file of papers shortly after work and arrived in good time for the meeting.

Until a couple of years after her mother's funeral, she had no idea that she had a half-brother. Since the age of three, Janet had been bought up by her mother alone after her father was killed in a road accident. Home was 2 Easton Drive for all of that time and with no other siblings and the mortgage paid off by her father's life insurance, although not well off, the Bassett girls, as they called themselves, were quite content and mother and daughter were always close.

At seventeen, when her mother suddenly died, the shock of her loss rocked her previously steady foundations. Now, of course, the house and what little money there was belonged to her and she had to grow up fast to deal with responsibilities that should not have troubled her young life.

When, just three weeks after her nineteenth birthday, the solicitor wrote to her to explain the approach they had received from someone claiming to be her half brother, her world was turned upside down again.

At first she was suspicious, but when he asked to meet she found her curiosity was aroused and she had to know more about this mysterious stranger that her mother had never mentioned at all.

Over the next ten or twelve months the story unfolded. Her half brother was over seven years her senior and the result of a liaison her mother had at the age of fifteen. As was the way in those days in an Irish Catholic household, the child was taken immediately into care and offered for adoption with a new identity.

It had taken him the best past of three years to track down any trace of his birth family, her half brother explained in his letters, and he was devastated to learn that he was too late to meet his real mother.

Janet was careful to do all the 'due diligence' she could think of and the solicitor who her new half-brother suggested they should use eventually confirmed in writing that he was indeed her half-brother. The fee he charged, even split two ways, was not cheap and Janet hoped her mother was right when she used to say 'You get what you pay for in life.'

Having it confirmed that she did indeed have a new family member was when she started to feel guilty.

Her comfortable life at 2 Easton Drive, albeit as part of a one parent family, was very different to his, and as she got to know him she realised he had missed out on so much.

He had been adopted by a postman and his wife and grew up somewhere in North London, attending a sting of secondary schools. His adoptive parents split up when he was fourteen and he went into foster care until he reached the age of sixteen, when he joined the Royal Navy. After that he ended up working in an insurance company in central London.

From what he said the job was not badly paid, but with the cost of living in London being so high, he lived in a tiny rented studio flat over the top of some garages in a noisy mews at the back of Holborn, from where he could walk to work.

At just nineteen years old, Janet was still quite impressionable, and when she visited the little studio flat, with her friend Lucy for support, she felt even more guilty about the life she had enjoyed in comparison to how her half-brother was obviously struggling.

Janet was due to go to university, but there had been no higher education opportunities for him, and now he seemed to be stuck in a rut.

He told her he had had girlfriends but never married and felt that now he was destined to remain single. He explained that he had a routine that suited him … breakfast at the greasy cafe on the corner, sandwiches for lunch at his desk, and a TV dinner before bed. He was, he said, happy enough with his life, but Janet could detect a restlessness in his eyes that she took for unhappiness.

There was one element of his life that he seemed to have under steady control, however. Working in the insurance industry he knew and understood the value of planning for the future and convinced Janet that they should insure each others' lives and protect themselves from hardship if illness in later life prevented them from being able to earn a living or support themselves. He did not, he said, want to be a burden to her or anyone else if the worst happened, and he was certainly in no position to support her if illness should affect her life.

It was a grim subject to discuss, he agreed, but they had to be sensible. At his age, and being that bit older than Janet, he wanted to protect her young life from any responsibility for him as he got older. It made some sense.

So, with help from a colleague in his office they drew up a Trust and took out 'critical health insurance with life cover' on each other. Janet had to make some economies to afford the premiums which, because of his age were not cheap, but she was still able to pursue her university career, at which she excelled and was soon being offered lucrative jobs when her studies finished.

Many years later, of course, the worst did happen.

A severe stroke cut Barry down and Janet found herself claiming on the long forgotten insurance policy to pay for his care.

Unfortunately the policy had not really kept pace with inflation and Janet, now successful in her career, found the Trustees who managed the investment process on her behalf needed her to top up the Trust fund to pay the care costs, so she mortgaged 2 Easton Drive to pay for it.

Although they did see a bit of each other initially, in the intervening years Janet and Barry had drifted apart somewhat. Now though, with the prognosis being terminal, and the costs having increased considerably, Janet felt a responsibility more acutely to support him, and she put 2 Easton Drive on the market to use some of the equity tied up there to make Barry's last years or months as comfortable as she could.

According to the Trustees, apart from the Trust fund they administered, as far as they knew he had only one other form of financial support in the form of a monthly payment, paid directly to the nursing home, which came from his employer, it was assumed, which covered an element, but not all of his care costs. The Trust itself bore the burden of the rest of it and although she had punctiliously paid in the agreed amount every month since it was set up, never missing a payment, funds were now running dangerously low.

Janet had to act, and the meeting with the Trustees was to arrange to ensure that one way or another all

Barry's care costs were covered from now on.

What happened when she got to the meeting, however, was a shock. The accountant who chaired the meeting asked her to sit down and told her that they had just heard from the nursing home that unfortunately Barry had passed away in the night.

-oOo-

As he sat with his coffee on one of the three, uncomfortable, blue, hessian-covered office chairs in the tiny main reception area, and looked at the domineering bar arrangement behind which the receptionist sat unseen, Orlando thought of the large welcoming reception area at the Madrid office of his father's firm where he often worked.

The polished marble floor and little groups of four or five black leather sofas arranged around glass coffee tables which greeted visitors as they stepped out of one of the two lifts, to be greeted by smiling smartly dressed girls and offered refreshment, was very different to this.

There wasn't even anywhere obvious to put his coffee down, other than a tiny table covered in dusty literature which looked as if it had lain there untouched for years.

The coffee, served, he noticed, in a mug, was awful instant stuff with a sludgy skin on the surface, and there had been no attempt to ask him how he preferred his drink. The choice was coffee or tea, with or without sugar and milk.

Orlando understood, with sparkling clarity now, the importance of first impressions.

-oOo-

While Orlando was detained with his coffee in the main reception, Dawn was standing uncertainly by her desk and being 'briefed' by the Senior Partner himself and the oily Mr Ledger, the office manager on what she had to do to make this locum welcome.

'You should make sure that the files of all the current cases are easily to hand as he will probably want to spend some time reading them before he does too much else, and for a while, until he is ready, it might be best if you don't make any appointments for people to see him' they explained.

-oOo-

Orlando's eyes roamed around the small area and took in the hunting scene hanging crookedly on the wall behind the receptionist's barricade and the down-at-heel furnishings he could just see in an empty office behind it, and he noticed how quiet it was.

In the London office, while the floor that was to be the new Conveyancing Department was currently mostly builder's debris and pallets, the rest of the building positively hummed with activity.

Granted, the conveyancing team only had two articled clerks and a couple of typists so far, who were currently working in spare offices at the back of the Civil Litigation department, but that was all due to change and there was a constant movement of people to and fro between offices and the various departments which gave the place a lively, vibrant feel.

Here, the building seemed to be sleeping.

Admittedly in London there were only twenty-five or thirty live cases being worked on currently and about ten of those involved a property developer client they worked with all around the world, but Orlando confidently expected 'his' floor of the London office block to soon be as buzzing and busy as the rest of the company, and he wondered, not for the first time whether offering to help out at Oakshott, Parslow & Partners, with some simple domestic conveyancing was going to hold his interest for very long.

-oOo-

'All clear on that?' asked Mr Ledger in his high-pitched adenoidal voice as soon as the Senior Partner's office door closed across the corridor.

'I think so,' said Dawn unhappily. She was not looking forward to what lay ahead and was still feeling nervous despite the pep talk. 'What is this guy's name, by the way?'

'Orlando Sanchez Fernandez,' intoned Mr Ledger, 'And the Senior Partner was telling me he is Spanish.'

Dawn clutched at the back of her office chair and felt one of her carefully manicured nails crack.

Orlando? Here? How could this be? Surely there couldn't be two people with that name around, could there?

No wait! Orlando said he worked for his father's firm and maybe they had the same name. They did that sort of thing abroad, didn't they? ... This would probably be the father then.

'Well you had better go down and get him. He is waiting in Reception,' said Mr Ledger, passing through the door to return to his own office, 'Remember I'm just over the corridor if you would like a hand or anything,' he leered, licking his lips as he took in Dawn's profile once more.

Dawn swallowed hard and realised she had a very dry throat and, she noticed with horror as she looked at her fingers, she had broken a nail.

She checked her reflection one last time in the dirty window and started down the stairs to meet Orlando Sanchez Fernandez.

-oOo-

Chapter 11

The receptionist slipped on her shoes and wobbled to her feet.

'Dawn,' she said, 'This is Mr ... erm ... Sanchez Fernandez.'

'I know,' said Dawn. 'We've met.'

Orlando's amused smile might be bewitching but now as it turned on the receptionist, it was cold and slightly superior.

'Yes. Dawn is a one of the students at the college I am from,' he said, 'so I have met before. Hello again, Dawn.'

Half pleased, half terrified, Dawn led the way up the narrow stairs to Mrs Patrick's office and asked Orlando how he was.

'I'm a doing just fine, Dawn, thank you. Now please, where are the other staff?'

Orlando seemed somewhat taken aback when she

explained that, until they got a new secretary, she was it, as far as staff went.

'There are no other staff? But you are a much too young to be qualified, no? How does Mrs Pauline cope with just you to help?'

Cheek! thought Dawn .. but then again it was a fair comment. It wasn't her fault she was young and unqualified.

'How many cases have you going on now?' Orlando was asking, 'And have you no clerks or case managers?'

'I'm training to be a Paralegal,' replied Dawn lamely.

'But if it is just a you, who does the real work? You are a school leaver, no? How can a chica, I mean young little girl, like you do this work?'

Dawn felt herself redden. Little girl? Just a School Leaver? Even allowing for differences in the language and translation this was sounding quite insulting. In a different environment, confronted with such statements, Dawn would have stamped her foot and started shouting at this point, but she was not at home in her father's house now, and she had to bite her tongue.

'How many people are there in the whole office?' Orlando asked.

Dawn thought for a moment.

'In the whole company I think there are about twenty-five people but only Mrs Patrick and I in Conveyancing.'

She pointed at the desk.

'Er, these are the files of the current cases we have here now. I got them all out for you.'

Orlando looked at the small pile and opened the cover of the first one.

'That's it?' he said, 'No more?'

'No more,' confirmed Dawn.

'Madre Mia!' said Orlando, 'No wonder they only need to employ children here!'

-oOo-

Geoff knew, of course, that his wife's sister wrote historical romantic novels, but he had no idea she was considered good enough to be asked to read them at some sort of literary event in Wales.

He had seen the books lying about when visiting Matravers Hall and knew there were even a couple gathering dust in a bookcase in his marital home, but he had never picked one up, let alone read any of them. They were not his sort of thing.

Now however he wondered if this stuff actually paid the bills at Matravers Hall. It was, after all, a big old place and its upkeep could not be cheap.

All he really knew about his sister-in-law's writing output was that Bobbie regarded it as utter bilge and hated to admit that her mother put her name to such things.

In earlier times, on one occasion when it emerged who her mother was, Bobbie was so affected that she ran away from school and had to be returned there by a policeman.
Whilst being delivered in a police car boosted her prestige considerably amongst her fellow schoolgirls, she always had a horror of having to confront her mother's profession and was at pains to avoid the subject at all times.

Geoff did not want to upset his sister-in-law but he did feel that now Bobbie was twenty-one, or was it twenty-two, she should be allowed at least some freedoms and her mother's over-protective methods were a bit much.
Granted that who could say where Bobbie's little adventures would lead, and episodes in the past did give him pause for thought, but she was grown up now and was entitled to live her own life.

To Geoff, a gentle cruise up and down a portion of the Thames in the company of some university friends seemed harmless enough and he resolved to do what he could to make it possible.

His first step was to call the lawyer handling his divorce at Oakshott, Parslow & Partners. If his plan worked, his wife would soon be scuttling back to the marital home with all speed.

After that he called Bobbie.

'Listen, Bobbie,' he said, when she answered her phone, 'Organising the split of money, property and what-not is one of the most difficult and stressful parts of getting a divorce and, once the lawyers get involved it only gets worse ...'

'Oh, Uncle Geoff, I'm sorry to hear that,' said Bobbie solicitously.

'Yes, well. But be that as it may, it could be that we can make use of the latest impasse the lawyers have engineered to delay things, which ups their fees of course, because the longer it takes from their point of view the better ...'

'I'm not sure I follow you ...' said Bobbie, scratching her head with the tip of the ballpoint pen she was holding, then, seeing what she had done, throwing the thing away from her in disgust.

'Allow me to explain, young Bobbie. On my behalf my lawyers have put it about that I'm cutting up rough about getting the house valued and putting it on the market. All nonsense of course, I just want the thing over and done with with the minimum of fuss and bother, but the fellow at the solicitors' says it has to be done like this to stop my wife selling it to any Tom, Dick or Harry at a knock-down price. She can't do anything about it until I say she can.'

'Good heavens, that's a bit mistrustful, isn't it?' said Bobbie.

'It's the lawyers way to sow doubt and antagonism like this, so that they can step in later and sort it all out … for a fee, of course.'

'It all seems very mercenary …' sympathised Bobbie.

'But we could possibly use it to your, and my advantage.'

'In what way?'

'Well, you see my wife, egged on by her solicitor, is now coming to the boil in frustration about what she has been told is my unwillingness to start the process of selling the house. The facts of the matter, let me say at this point, are quite the reverse of that. This must go no further, Bobbie, but Janet and I are looking to buy a house together, so of course I need to get my share of the sale of the house to make that happen. I can rely on your discretion on that point, can't I Bobbie? I must insist on it remaining just between us.'

'My lips are sealed, Uncle Geoff, 'and even if they put matchsticks between my little toes I shall never tell.' Bobbie stated.

'Matchsticks between your toes? Whatever are you talking about, Bobbie? Why would anyone put matchsticks between your toes?'

'Well, I've no idea actually. I wondered at first if it

was anything to do with painting one's toenails when I heard mother reading aloud something about it from one of her books. But then I realised that the baddies, in mother's book I mean, proposed to light the matches to obtain a confession as to where the hero had hidden the keys of the safe, when the flames burned down and caused him discomfort. A silly idea, I thought, when a swift sock on the breezer would bring faster results and add a satisfactory increase to the amount of blood already being sprayed about in that particular section of mother's novel.'

'Yes, well, as I was saying,' said Geoff shaking his head. 'Supposing I let it be known that I was prepared to allow her to get the estate agents in as long as she undertook to handle showing them around, given that my solicitor has put it out that I find it too painful to visit the place which holds so many upsetting memories for me…'

'And I thought the plots of my mothers books were rotten …' interjected Bobbie.

'If, as I was saying, I insisted that she based herself at the house to meet the estate agents and handle viewings and so on, I believe she would rush back there like greased lightning and you would be released from your Auntie-sitting responsibilities …'

'Uncle Geoff, you are a wonder! That is pure genius. If my mother could think up clever things like that to put in her books to enable the lovers to meet, she would have them queuing round the block to buy the beastly things!'

'Lovers queuing round the block?' Geoff chuckled.

'No, punters, customers, book buyers, silly! The lovers only meet on paper, but the readers part with hard cash to read about them. Mad isn't it.'

'If it pays the bills …'

'Oh Uncle Geoff, you are so clever! I can't see how this wheeze can fail. You have made your favourite niece-by-marriage a very happy young lady. I'm afraid I must go now and do joyful dances on the lawn before I phone my friend Brice-Waterman and tell him we are on, and I shall soon be draping myself decorously on the prow, or is it the transom, of his elegant river cruiser in the sunshine! Thank you, Uncle Geoff. You are still my knight in shining Jaguar after all!'

-oOo-

Chapter 12

Back in the office now, but only for a visit, Pauline sat uncomfortably in the Senior Partner's room. Barry's Will was simple enough, he left everything to Pauline and she remembered that they had set up matching Wills when they married, but the Senior Partner also had letter which had been lodged later with the Wills without her knowledge.

The Senior Partner looked uncomfortable as he handed Pauline a photocopy of this letter and began to read the original out loud.

"Dearest Pauline," it started innocuously enough, "When you read this I will no longer be able to be at your side, but there are a few things I can still do to make your life a little more comfortable.

"You will recall that I was adopted from birth in Dublin, but it has been my life's mission to find my birth mother, if she is still alive and make sure that she knew I existed.

"I have had some success in this, and although I have

been unable to get conclusive proof that any of the persons I identified is actually my mother, I have got as close as I can and one of those on the list is almost certainly my mother, although which one I cannot say.

"I traced these people through research at the insurance company where I worked and had access to various records, as well as elsewhere, using public records. I have visited most of them a few years back before we met. Some, however, have passed away, although I have made contact with their relatives where possible.

"Surprisingly, one of those relatives lives quite close to our house and details of my relationship with her will become clear shortly.

You need to know that certain papers are contained in the smaller of the two packing cases (the sealed one) I put in the loft when I moved in with you.

There you will find a ledger in which I have recorded details of each person, the financial settlement or arrangement I reached with them and how to access the fixed assets and funds.

"If you are reading this you will by now be aware that all my so called 'worldly goods' become yours on my death and I have to tell you now that you will also need to ask your lawyer to obtain access to two bank accounts and locate the deeds of a property. The details of all that are also in the sealed packing case.

"I hope unravelling this does not cause you too much

difficulty and I have done my best to make it easy to follow as you will see. I know you will think it odd that I appear to have been living a double life, at least before I met you, but I have always thought that if you found out about what I had been doing it would destroy our relationship. To me, actually finding someone who loved me at last has been the most precious thing and I have not wanted to do anything put that at risk.

"Marrying you was certainly the highlight of my life, Pauline, and my love will always be with you."

There then followed some instructions for the solicitor as to where he wanted his ashes scattered and his preference for a simple cremation rather than a funeral.

-oOo-

The nice policewoman asked if there was anyone she could call to help her.

Initially she could not think of anyone. She did not make friends easily and she and Barry had been so wrapped up in each other they didn't seem to need anyone else.

At last it occurred to her that old Mr Shotter from the office was really the only person she knew well enough to ask. Since he had retired and only lived around the corner, he might be able to spare her a little time.

To her surprise the policewoman said she would contact him, break the news about Barry's death and ask if he was prepared to lend a hand.

It was fortunate that Mr Shotter responded positively, given that the first thing they had to do was get the small sealed packing case out of the loft and examine its contents, and Pauline doubted if she could do it on her own.

Although the Senior Partner thought it would be wise, she had not told the police about the sealed packing case yet, and she decided to tell Mr Shotter first.

Dressed as she had never seen him before, in saggy corduroy trousers and a crumpled open necked shirt, rather than a suit, Mr Shotter stood on Pauline's doorstep within the hour.

His gentle features and kind concerned smile were such a welcome sight that Pauline quite unexpectedly found herself in tears. It was the first time she had allowed herself to really cry since Barry died.

-oOo-

Fortunately there was a loft ladder attached to the hatch although it was still a struggle for Pauline and Mr Shotter to manhandle the packing case down into the light.

They paused for breath when they had the heavy and unbalanced thing on the landing carpet, and Pauline realised she should have thought to put a cloth down first as it was covered in cobwebs and quite dusty.

'Well, from what you have told me, Pauline,' Mr Shotter said, straightening up with his hands on the small of his back, 'the sooner we get this wretched thing open and take a look inside, the better.'

Pauline looked at the box. It had once been a tea-chest, she suspected, and had sharp metal strips around the edges. The lid was nailed shut and she was surprised when Mr Shotter drew a garden trowel from his back pocket and said, 'Shall I see if I can lever the top up?'

-oOo-

That night when Dawn DeSantos got home she ran straight up to her room, buried her head in her pillow and wept.

What beasts men could be, she thought.

If it wasn't the slimy Mr Ledger ogling her, it was that rude pig Orlando bossing her about and treating her like a child.

She hated being on her own with either of them in the office and for a fleeting moment she wished she still had her pony so she could take it for a good hard ride to release her tensions.

There was a knock at her door.

'Go away!' she shouted, although she didn't mean it.

'It's me, Stefano, the front door was open and I heard you crying.'

Stefano was her second cousin and was employed in the restaurant in charge of 'front of house'.

'I came to see your father, but he is not here, I think. Are you all right, Dawn?'

Dawn tried to pull herself together. She liked Stefano and they had pretty much grown up together so had few secrets.
She dabbed her eyes with a tissue and went to the door.

-oOo-

'The trouble with boats,' Bobbie explained as she sat in Janet's lounge, 'is that they are sometimes hired by brash young men who just want to go from pub to riverside pub getting drunk.'

'Your trip didn't come up to your expectations then then?' asked Geoff solicitously.

'If you mean did it fulfil the hopes of a young girl who imagined it as a halcyon idyll drifting along the river, trailing a delicate hand in the water perhaps, as she watched the dappled sunlight play romantically upon the clear water, then no, it did not.'

'Oh dear.'

'"Oh, dear," is right, Uncle Geoff. And it wasn't just

the boys. The boat was damp and old and in need of several coats of paint. It was also considerably smaller than the young ocean liner Brice-Waterman described in his sales talk, and it rocked about alarmingly inducing a certain green tinge to invade my healthy tan.'

'So you came home early.'

'I abandoned my shipmates with a none-too-cheery wave when we reached Chertsey Lock and I shared a taxi with Rosy straight here.'

'Rosy didn't stick it either then?'

'Not all the Brice-Waterman family are uncouth oafs, Rosy at least has a little taste.'

'Well, Janet will be here any minute so you can meet someone else who has taste. Would you like another cup of tea?'

Geoff was not in the least surprised that Bobbie's little adventure had come unstuck. It was quite the normal form for her, but he had not expected her to turn up at 2 Easton Drive.

'Yes, please,' said Bobbie, 'and then I must not impose on your hospitality. After meeting Janet, which I am looking forward to, I shall establish which is the best train to Wiltshire and trouble you for a lift to the station, if you wouldn't mind.'

'Don't you think it is a bit late to be considering

travelling alone on a train, Bobbie? I'm sure Janet wouldn't mind if you stayed here tonight and went back in the morning.'

'Well, I wouldn't like to be in the way, but if you think …'

'I'm sure it will be no problem.'

'And is there a hot shower that has room to swing your arms and doesn't rock about alarmingly or smell of duckweed?'

'I believe so, although I would have to check, as I don't use the guest one myself.'

'Then that's settled then. I shall lay my pretty head here tonight and depart refreshed and ready to face life again on the morrow. Where are we going for dinner?'

-oOo-

Rosalind met Helen again at Miriam's Tea Rooms, by the recreation ground, but this time just for coffee.

'That nasty little Jonathan Ellis didn't like it when we told him we were not going to take his mortgage or insurance out, and Mike said he got quite rude on the phone.'

'You made Mike make the call then?'

'Well, yes, of course, in my condition I should avoid stress.'

'Rosalind, honestly, you are about two and a half minutes pregnant and a fit as a flea!'

'In between being sick, you mean. Coming here was a bit of a risk, but I didn't think there could possibly be anything left inside me to bring up, so I thought I would risk it.'

'Yes, well, moving on from that before I start chucking up too, who are you going to use as your solicitors. Will you being going to see Pauline?'

'What! After they made me redundant? I wouldn't give them the satisfaction! And anyway the vendor is already using them, so we can't.'

'I see.'

'No, we shall use the ones the mortgage broker put us onto. They are a licensed conveyancing company rather than solicitors, but the difference in fees is astonishing.'

'Pauline won't like that. Do you remember she used to call them "Poundshop pretenders". She thinks all conveyancing should be carried out by professional solicitors as it always used to be done.'

'Well, times have changed. And Pauline Patrick was way to much in the image of old Shotter to ever contemplate anything resembling modern life. I wonder if the office is still like something out of Dickens? Remember that silly date thing on the desk and the weird pencil sharpener?'

'What I remember is having to wind up that revolting green clock on the mantlepiece with half the handle of the key missing. I broke more nails on that than I care to remember!'

'Sorry, Helen, I haven't told you before, but I broke that key when it was my job to wind the wretched thing before you joined.'

'Well, that's our friendship ruined,' laughed Helen, 'I shall never speak to you again!'

The two women laughed at their little joke and then, as Rosalind announced she was not sure she could hold onto the coffee much longer, they said their goodbyes and as Helen sauntered back to work Rosalind made haste for her flat.

-oOo-

'It's coming now,' said Mr Shotter, repositioning his trowel, 'This ought to do it …'

With a crack of splintering wood the lid of the packing case gave up the fight and sprang free of its moorings.

Pauline had to force herself to look.

Inside, on top of a lot of paper, was an old fashioned manual typewriter.

'Ah,' said Mr Shotter, 'Thats why it was so heavy. Shall I lift it out?'

-oOo-

Although she would never have dreamed of showing her tear-stained face in public, she didn't mind with Stefano. They had even been bathed together as kids.

Dawn opened the door and fell into his arms.

'All men are brutes,' she declared, and then thinking about what she had just said, 'Present company excepted.'

'I think you had better tell me all about it,' said Stefano, walking her to the bed and sitting down next to her.

-oOo-

As predicted Bobbie and Janet got on like a house on fire which took her mind off the death of her brother.

Janet said she agreed entirely that Brice-Waterman was not fit for human consumption and volunteered Geoff to drive Bobbie back to Wiltshire in the morning.

'We have to keep these old retirees busy,' she said, 'otherwise they might go off.'

There were gales of laughter in the pizza house as they ate and the two of them regaled each other with tales of their youth and, mostly in Bobbie's case it must be said, tales of unfortunate incidents with boys.

At one point, when Bobbie went for another go at the salad cart, Janet said,
'Isn't she a scream! Why don't we ask her to stay the weekend so she goes home on the day she would have done if she hadn't left the boat?'

Geoff let a mild exclamation escape before he caught himself.

'But you don't know what she is like! She is bound to start something!'

'Not under your watchful eye … oh, here she comes … Bobbie, why don't you stay with us for the weekend and go back on Monday as you originally planned? I assume you have enough clothes and if not I would think we are mostly about the same size, or there is always the washing machine …'

Geoff, powerless now to resist the tidal wave of excited women who pretty shortly, he was sure, would start talking about going shopping together, sidled off to the salad cart to be alone.

-oOo-

With a final heave, the typewriter was out.

'Phew! That's a heavy old thing!' exclaimed Mr Shotter.

'You mind your back,' said Pauline, peering into the packing case.

'What are you expecting to find in there, Pauline? It's not the old typewriter you were after, I assume.'

Pauline reached in and pulled out a handful of blank pages of 'headed notepaper' from some solicitor in Wales as she started to tell Mr Shotter about the letter, and her visits from the police before and after Barry died.

-oOo-

It took Sylvia three days to incinerate the magazines properly.

The incinerator worked superbly, it had to be said, and fortunately did not make much smoke, which considering her neighbours might want to put washing out was a blessing.

She even thought about retrieving Bryn's copies of Fifty Shades and the Khama Sutra from the bin and burning those, but as the bin was due to be emptied, they lay under other rubbish, so she decided to abandon that plan.

The hot ashes left in the bottom were left to cool on the final day as she went in for a well-earned drink. She would leave the incinerator for the young couple buying the house, she thought. They probably didn't have that sort of thing.
And then there was the lawn mower and the garden tools and so on; she would have no use for them now.

Sylvia looked in the envelope for the form Mrs Patrick had given her on which she was expected to write what she was leaving, and if she wanted to sell some it, how much for.

When you came to think about it there was all sorts of stuff she could leave that a young couple just starting out might find useful. She didn't need them and she didn't really want to charge any money for them, so she took out a pen and began listing the items.

The washing machine was one thing, and the fridge freezer, and probably the cooker, although that was gas and they might prefer electric …

As she toiled over the form, next doors' cat, who until recently had been a frequent visitor, was foiled in his attempts to get through the cat flap which had now been sealed shut by the addition of a screw through the frame.

With a growl of frustration he stalked off to inspect the incinerator which was radiating a not unpleasant warmth.

-oOo-

There were two old fashioned ledgers of the sort with metal hinges and hard covers in the bottom of the packing case.

Mr Shotter and Pauline had moved them onto the dining table to get a better look at them and they were very surprised by what they found.

The thinner of the two books had an index on the front page which read as follows ...

Section 1: Gertrude Sampson ... £5,000 one off payment and confirmation letter.

Section 2: Elizabeth Joyce O'Leary ... Now deceased. Policy sold.

Section 3: Mary Eileen Maloney ... Deceased, one daughter. Trust policy.

Section 4: Susan Smith ... No records found.

Section 5: Sybil Jane O'Reilly ... Family welcome. Now deceased. Hotel freehold.

Section 6: Siobhan O'Toole ... £1,000 monthly allowance.

Quite what all that meant was not clear until they opened the second larger ledger.

There they found the book divided into sections and in each section a series of diary notes and a description, updated many times with crossings out and re-writes of the research Barry had done to find each of the women, and if he found them, the arrangements he had reached with them if they met.

There were copies of Birth and Death certificates and various papers and newspaper clippings, some of which related to an adoption agency in Dublin.

According to the notes, the first name on the list,

Gertrude Sampson, had given him very short shrift and made him sign a legal agreement, which was clipped into the file. That agreement stated that in return for a 'goodwill payment' of £5,000, he would make no further claim of any sort against her and would henceforth leave her alone, never mentioning to anyone that they had ever met.

The second name, Elizabeth Joyce O'Leary, had rather more paperwork in her section. The diary notes set out several meetings and Barry seemed to come away having sold her an insurance policy, the brief terms of which were recorded in the file. Pauline and Mr Shotter were astonished to read that the policy had paid out on her death, a little over three years since they met, and she had left Barry a £15,000 inheritance.

And so it went on, listing Barry's research, trips to meet people and details of what he extorted from them.

Perhaps the most astounding item from Pauline's point of view was that the paperwork for Sybil Jane O'Reilly seemed to be indicating that after her death she had left Barry the freehold of a Hotel in Ballybunion, County Kerry, Ireland, which was let to a well-known hotel chain operator and produced an income of £51,000 a year.

'Good gracious,' said Mr Shotter, 'If, as you say, Barry left everything to you in his Will, it seems you now own a hotel!'

'I had absolutely no idea about any of this,' spluttered Pauline, choking back the tears, 'I think we had better call the police.'

-oOo-

Chapter 13

It was usual to have a lesson first.

Martin supposed that was to help calm the nerves, although in his case it wasn't really working. He had already mounted the kerb when he messed up backing round a corner while practising, and now the time for the driving test itself had arrived.

The examiner was short, thin and angry looking, with a tiny little black moustache under his prominent nose and a clipboard in his hand. He was walking with a stiff gait towards Martin and his instructors car now.

'Good afternoon,' said Martin.

'Yes, well, come round to the front of the car and look at that car there. Can you read the number plate?'

And so it went on. Martin concentrating as hard as he could and the little man looking at him suspiciously and making occasional marks on his clipboard.

When it was over, at last, and he asked Martin to turn the engine off, they sat in silence for what seemed like hours as the examiner looked at his clipboard and Martin tried not to scream.

'There are several points you need to attend to, but you have passed,' he said.

Martin looked at the little man in a new light. He saw now that he had been quite mistaken and his was a most distinguished moustache. Should Martin shake his hand? No, the instructor might see how much his hand was shaking.

'Thank you very much, sir,' he said instead, and he meant every word of it.

-oOo-

Given that she had not heard from Oakshott, Parslow and Partners, since her embarrassing visit when poor little Dawn broke down in tears, Sylvia had no idea if they had found and appointed someone to do the conveyancing work yet.

The only way to find out was to deliver that form back and ask, and as she selected her smoke grey wrap-around shawl from the cupboard and slipped on her shoes, her heart was light and she knew she had done the right thing, gifting all that stuff to the young couple buying the house without looking for payment.

There was a lot of it, and the more she thought about it the more she found she could add. What need had she of such things as bedside cabinets and ironing boards where she was going? She was sure all that sort of thing would be provided at the country house she would be living in, and she remembered that the furniture in the guest room, when she went for a brief stay, had been of a far better quality than the flat-pack stuff she was leaving behind at the house.

She thought how grateful she would have been when she and Bryn were starting out if someone had given them plates and bowls, glasses and cutlery; and it gave her a warm glow to think how pleased the young couple would be that they didn't have to buy all that sort of thing straight away.

Even if it wasn't to their taste, she reasoned, having lampshades, bedding, saucepans, a television and such like already in place would give them a start, and they could replace them as they went along if they wanted to.

Sylvia hummed a little tune as she walked to the solicitor's office.

-oOo-

'My condolences for your loss,' said DS Morris a little stiffly, 'Are these ledgers through here?'

The police had been at the house for hours now, looking in cupboards and drawers, under beds, and even in the garden.

The Senior Partner had arrived a little earlier and examined some of the documents, taking photographs with his mobile phone of some bank statements and papers they found in the packing case, and discussing what they were doing with the police.

DS Morris now joined the throng and, as the senior officer, took charge.

'There is one thing I can tell you, Mrs Patrick,' said DS Morris. 'A deceased person cannot be charged with murder, so the claim Barry made before he died about your mother's death can now be largely ignored. However, I have to tell you that we will need to be in contact with our opposite numbers in other forces, in Ireland particularly, to ascertain how those persons on the list there died. I'm sure that will all be routine and will turn out to be 'natural causes' in each case, but you understand that we must still check as there is something called the Forfeiture law which does not allow a person who kills another to benefit from their death. Now I'm not saying that that applies here, of course, but we do have to tick the box.'

Pauline looked at DS Morris uncomprehendingly. This was all getting a bit much for her.

Mr Shotter had now been at the house with Pauline for many hours, but he stayed on to see her through this ordeal as best he could. In between helping that nice policewoman make tea for everyone, he sat with Pauline as the police picked through her house around her.

'It's very kind of you to stay with me, Mr Shotter,' said Pauline, 'and I do appreciate it, but if you need to go home I will completely understand. Now that all these police are here I certainly won't be lonely.'

'It is no bother at all, Pauline, and there is nothing spoiling at home. Since I retired life has been rather quiet.'

Mr Shotter didn't say so, of course, but this was the most excitement he had had for several months, and he didn't want to miss the mystery unfolding.

'Now,' DS Morris was saying, 'You are quite sure that you have no knowledge at all of these bank accounts? There is quite a lot of money passing through them and it seems odd that you should not have had any idea that this was going on.'

'I promise you, Detective, that the first I knew about this was when that letter was read out to me in the office. This is all a huge shock to me.' Pauline dabbed her eyes with the sodden tissue she held. 'I wish none of this had happened.'

'Try not to get upset, Pauline, dear,' said Mr Shotter. 'You know they are only doing their job.'

-oOo-

When they returned from their shopping trip, Bobbie and Janet were buzzing.

'We have so much in common, Uncle Geoff,' twittered Bobbie, as Janet unloaded the car, 'I am so glad you have found such a lovely person. She told me all about the time she, like me, was left unloved and abandoned on the shelf and what she did about it. Do you think

I've got nice teeth, Uncle Geoff? You don't think a little cosmetic assistance might help here and there,' she said, baring her teeth at him.

'Oh, don't be silly, Bobbie,' said Geoff, recoiling, 'You have fine straight teeth and a lovely smile. Maybe a little less garlic with your lunch would help though!'

'Whoops! Sorry about that. We found this lovely little tagliatelle restaurant near the mall, and well, there was this yummy garlic oil and it seemed rude not to!'

'You have enough bags there for a month's worth of supermarket shopping,' said Geoff as Janet heaved the last of the bags into the already full hall and balanced them on the stairs.

'We didn't go supermarket shopping, Geoff. This is all clothes!' smiled Janet in her disarming way.

'Oh, then what is for supper?' he asked.

'That depends where you are taking us,' said Bobbie, 'I fancy a steak!'

'What! After all that pasta? You must have hollow legs, Roberta,' giggled Janet.

'I fancy a steak too,' said Geoff, but the girls were taking the bags upstairs and discussing the contents, so nobody was listening.

-oOo-

'My God, look at all this stuff!' exclaimed Mike, 'It's like she has dumped the entire contents of her house on us!'

Rosalind had read the email from the solicitor earlier and been shocked at what the vendor was going to be leaving in the house. She looked around the flat they rented 'unfurnished' and could not find anything that the list did not duplicate, except something called an incinerator, whatever that was, a lawn mower and some garden tools.

'What are we going to do, Mike? We don't want to appear rude, but if she doesn't need it, isn't this all stuff she should be taking to the tip or giving to charity? I think she is just leaving it to us to sort out!'

-oOo-

As Mr Shotter dozed in Barry's armchair and Pauline fidgeted, the police continued their searches.

Unfortunately, the nice police lady had gone off duty, to be replaced by an older woman who was a little off-hand, but at least kept the tea coming. She explained that she would be staying all night and mentioned that Pauline was not being held under caution or any thing like that but shouldn't go out until the current 'situation' had been resolved.

Pauline was beginning to feel that this was some never-ending nightmare from which she could not escape.

She wanted to scream, but Mr Shotter woke up and

squeezed her hand reassuringly.

-oOo-

Chapter 14

Martin was delighted, of course.

His father had found that someone in the office was changing his wife's car and was prepared to sell it to him for an attractive price.

Martin would have to pay his father back over many months and the insurance cost was eye-watering, but the dark blue Volkswagen Golf now sitting outside looked splendid, and he had already washed and polished it and hoovered out the inside.

It was hardly the latest model, of course, but the Volkswagen Golf hadn't really changed much since it first came out, so unless you parked it next to a newer one, nobody would notice its age. It was in pretty good condition too, having spent at least the past ten years with the previous owners, since they bought it secondhand, in a garage when not in use.

It did have 120,000 miles on the clock and a few scratches and dents, but it polished up well enough and Martin was really pleased with it.

'Can I drive you there, Mr Brownlow?' he asked now.

Stiffhams had received 'instructions' to measure up and value a house not far from the office and he was keen to put his new car to work.

'Well, yes, all right. I suppose so,' said Mr Brownlow, 'So long as you go carefully and don't drive too fast. There is plenty of time and no need to rush.'

Mr Brownlow knew about young men in motor cars and how they could get carried away and he realised he was taking his life in his hands.

-oOo-

The next day, by lunchtime, all the police had gone and Pauline had a phone call from the Senior Partner asking her to go in to discuss the various papers he had examined and what they meant.

Mr Shotter had not gone home the previous night until after nine o'clock and although he had phoned this morning to see how she was and offer his services again, she did not really think she could impose on him to go with her to the meeting, much as she appreciated his support.

She was shown into the Senior Partner's room a little after four o'clock, and after some preliminaries he got down to business.

'We have established contact with the bank and now that we have the Death Certificate, they have been able to give us some details of what Barry was doing with his accounts there,' he explained. 'I must admit that the picture is somewhat complicated and more information on some items is awaited, however, what we do know so far is that there is a substantial credit balance in one of the accounts on which interest is being paid into the other. The other account is operated like a current account with a series of standing orders going out, and income coming in.'

'Whatever was he doing?' Pauline asked.

'Well, I can tell you that he made a regular payment of £1,000 a month to a care home in a suburb of Dublin to contribute to the care of a Miss Siobhan O'Toole, and paid £300 a month into a Trust fund, the details of which are awaited. In terms of income the account shows an annual payment received of the equivalent of £51,000 in Euros from a hotel chain, and a credit balance of some £170,000.'

'My God!' said Pauline, 'Such a a lot of money!'

'Well, yes, and there are also several other small monthly amounts received from Barry's employers; commission, we would assume, which total up to … let me see … ah yes, £430 a month,' he said and shuffled some papers on his desk.

'The other point we have been able to establish, Pauline, is that a Sybil Jane O'Reilly left Barry the freehold of a hotel in Ballybunion … which I confess we thought was a rather unlikely name and had to look it up … but it does exist and is in County Kerry,

Ireland.'

'He never said anything to me about any of this…'

'No, well, if I may … that hotel investment produces the £51,000 annual income I mentioned earlier, which seems to be the bedrock of this financial … er, I nearly said jiggery-pokery … but you understand what I mean.'

'You said he paid out for the care of one of these people … could that be his mother?'

'It might be, but as he said in the letter I read you, he was not able to establish which of those on the list was actually his mother.'

'And what is this trust fund all about that he was making regular payments into?'

'Ah, that is one of the items we await more information on. So far we only know this Trust is, or rather was, paying a substantial proportion of the nursing home costs for Barry's care under the signature of someone called Janet Bassett. She could just be a professional Trustee administering it, of course and as yet that is all we know.'

'Barry kept mentioning a Janet. He even called me Janet a couple of times, but I thought nothing of it because of the dementia.'

'You must realise that you cannot access any of this or gain control of the accounts until Probate has been granted, and given the ... ah, complications with the involvement of the police, that may take some time. Presumably, though, you are happy for me to proceed to process that on your behalf....'

'Yes of course,'

'And set our fees off against the estate when resolved ...'

'Yes, fine.

'Are you all right, Pauline?'

'No, not really, and I'm not sure I ever will be again,' said Pauline, 'Are we done here? I think I would rather like to go home now.'

-oOo-

Chapter 15

Geoff's plan had worked and his wife had returned home and called in the estate agents immediately.

Whilst Bobbie's little trip was made possible, that excursion had not turned out well for her.
Bobbie seemed quite happy about it though and having roundly damned her shipmates and spent three nights with Janet and Geoff, she was in good spirits.

Janet was expected to work on the first day, of course, but the weekend was spent in a blur of trips out for meals here, and afternoon tea there, and of course shopping in between whiles. Bobbie had certainly made a friend and was keen to arrange to come to see them again as soon as practical.

Geoff was glad for his two favourite girls, especially as it distracted Janet from thinking too much about her late brother, but he did rather feel out of it when they got their heads together like a couple of excited schoolgirls, and he was quietly glad as he waved Bobbie off on the train.

At the moment the train pulled out of the station, Martin was carefully pulling up outside Geoff's house with Mr Brownlow in the passenger seat, all ready to meet his wife and begin the process of selling his house.

Martin remembered meeting her before, some months ago, and showing her round 2 Easton Drive. At the time she did not seem interested in moving house at all and Martin wondered what had changed.

-oOo-

Pauline was understandably grief stricken when Barry died and her agony was only increased when the police took an interest in her mother's death and then revealed that there were several women who also needed to be interviewed about his demise.

For Janet however, matters were even more complicated and she was called to another meeting with the Trustees to discuss the situation. This meeting was also attended by two policemen.

There was news about Barry's financial position to be digested, which although she was not given any real detail, the Detective informed her was very different to what she initially had been led to believe, all those years ago.

The accountant who always chaired the Trustee meetings explained that once Probate had been granted, the joint Life Insurance Policy she and Barry had set up to benefit each other would pay out handsomely, which would cover a considerable amount of what she had paid out over the years, but the separate Trust fund was now very much of interest to the police and their investigations were ongoing.

Apart from erratic and sporadic Christmas and birthday cards, Janet and Barry had drifted apart somewhat in the years since the Trust fund was established and the Detective had to bring her up to date with events.

Janet had no idea that Barry had married and she was surprised and a little annoyed that she had not been informed, let alone invited to the ceremony. But the most difficult thing she had to wrestle with was the doubt the policeman had sown in her mind as to whether she really was Barry's sister.

It emerged that what she thought was a pension from his employer that paid an element of his care costs was in fact a payment made by this wife she had never met, and the Trust fund she had assiduously paid into for years was bearing the main cost of his care.

She had to top this fund up on several occasions to deal with the spiralling cost of his nursing care over the last eighteen months as the balance in the account got gradually eaten away.

Now that the police had thrown doubt about whether

she and Barry were in fact related, the whole thing seemed as though it might be one enormous con, and she felt betrayed and more than a little foolish.

Admittedly the joint life insurance policy she took out on his life and her own, when it paid out, would pay back pretty much all that had been lost and that was a comfort; but she wondered about the enigma that was Barry Patrick and why he had done all this.

That was simple, DS Morris explained when Geoff, accompanying her to the meeting for moral support, asked that very question.

'Barry Patrick was a life-long gambler,' he revealed, 'The commissions he received from all these little life insurance policies he sold over the years supported his gambling habit and allowed him to indulge his passion for horse racing.'

DS Morris gave a little cough at this point and paused to draw breath.

'The remarkable thing was that, although he was not the most successful of horse racing punters, his income and expenditure more or less balanced out and he has not left any debts behind.'

-oOo-

It took over a week to get the information back from the police in Ireland, but when it arrived on DS Morris' desk, he read it all with growing interest.

Barry Patrick, it seemed was not just out for what he could get, but also had a caring side.

DS Morris had to refresh his mind on the contents of Section 6 of the ledgers which now occupied a corner of his desk. That related to a Sybil Jane O'Reilly who, Barry's notes revealed was in her late eighties and lived in a care home in Ireland.
From what he could gather, Barry had visited this lady several times over the years and it seemed that he formed a close bond with her. The notes made it clear that she had never married but had had a child out of wedlock which had been put up for adoption.

When, a dozen years ago, she moved from a little rented property into the care home where she still lived, Barry, presumably convinced that he was that child, had taken pity on her and arranged to pay £1,000 per month to the charity which ran the home for her care.

The local police had tried to interview her but their report put it rather curtly that her advanced age had bought on Altzhiemer's and it was not possible to get anything much of any use out of her.

It was also not clear if the payments would be able to continue now that Barry had died, but DS Morris passed that point up the line for others to deal with. In his experience it would take them ages to get round to doing anything about it, by which time the situation might be less unclear.

The police in Ballybunion also confirmed that there was indeed a hotel there, run and managed by a big group. They had spoken to the manager who had directed them to the head office who, on enquiry had confirmed that rent was paid to the freeholder. That dealt with Section 5 in the ledger.

Of Mary Eileen Maloney, who featured in Section 3, the Irish police could find no trace but it said 'Trust policy' in Barry's index and mentioned her marriage to a John Bassett and the subsequent birth of Janet Bassett, with whom they were already in contact. They knew some of the facts on that one, if not the whole picture.

It emerged that of those others on the list there was little or nothing to be found, although the Dublin police did pass on one bit of information about Gertrude Sampson, who featured in Section 1. She they said, was now married to a prominent secular senior media official within the Irish Catholic Church. No wonder she had made that so called 'goodwill payment' and made Barry sign a 'confidentiality agreement' stating that he would make no further claim or have any more contact with her.

What did emerge however, was that none of those on the list who had died had done so in suspicious circumstances. At least as far as those Barry had made contact with in search of his mother.

Elizabeth Joyce O'Leary had died of natural causes

three years after Barry had obviously met her and sold her a life insurance policy which, according to her Will, enabled her to leave him £15,000. The local police said there was nothing suspicious about her arrangements with Barry who had befriended her over several months and according to the notes in Section 2 of the ledger, he had visited her many times.

So, all in all, it did not appear that any menaces were used to extort money and in some respects Barry's arrangements with these women actually helped them out.

The only slightly odd thing was the Janet Bassett Trust fund, which still needed some explaining. Why had Barry kept paying into it and was there more than met the eye to his relationship with Janet Bassett.

He wondered if the incident leading to Pauline Patrick's mother's death, if it had actually happened, had been the start of Barry's problems with dementia. Could it be that he thought causing her death, and Pauline subsequently inheriting her house, was in some twisted way an attempt to help her financially? The problem with that element of this strange man's activities was that there was no way to prove that what he said had happened was true, and as such he the thought a judge, learning of Barry's mental heath, would throw out any case and say Barry was fantasising.

DS Morris sighed and put the file aside. There was now a complex and difficult report to write up with nothing much to show for all the time and resources used.

-oOo-

Chapter 16

Sylvia wondered what on earth was she going to do with all her stuff?

She had heard back from the lawyer that her buyers didn't want any of it apart from the lawn mower, the garden tools and the incinerator. It had not occurred to her that the young couple may already have everything else.

Things were so different now. When she and Bryn married they had absolutely nothing and apart from a hand-me-down mattress on the floor, lived in an unfurnished house for the first few weeks of their life together. She was only trying to help, but now it occurred to her that she would have to dispose of the contents of her house and she was not sure where to start.

She decided to phone Margaret at the retreat in Wales to give her an update and to ask, so that she could be sure, exactly what was provided in the room that was to be hers.

It was fortunate that she did.

-oOo-

As Martin and Mr Brownlow went through their now well-practised procedure for measuring a house up, Martin couldn't help noticing how keen the lady seemed to point out all the features and impress on them what a nice house it was.

This was all very different from the viewing at 2 Easton Drive when it seemed she couldn't get away from the place fast enough.

As Mr Brownlow took pictures at the end of the tour, things became a little clearer, but also more intriguing when she said that she needed a copy of the valuation sent to her ex-husband, whose address was 2 Easton Drive.

Martin blushed as he remembered that viewing. It didn't result in a sale, but it did lead to a romance. Martin imagined what it would be like if he got commission for acting as cupid and nearly laughed out loud at the thought of it.

-oOo-

Rosalind opened the door to Helen and invited her in.

She had decided it would be better if they met at the flat in case she had to rush to the loo unexpectedly.

Helen was almost invisible behind a huge parcel wrapped in paper featuring blue and pink babies sitting on white fluffy clouds.

'For you,' she said, pitching the huge parcel onto the sofa, 'Sorry about the paper, believe it or not that was all they had. I don't think Waitrose get much call for baby stuff.'

'What on earth …' said Rosalind, 'You didn't have to …'

'Oh, just open it, woman, it is only a silly thing and I haven't just staggered all the way down the High Street with it just to plonk it on your sofa!'

Rosalind did as she was told and revealed an enormous bale of paper nappies, which of course made the two friends burst into happy laughter.

'You silly sausage! It will be months before those will fit the baby. They are age three months plus!'

Helen looked more closely at the packaging.

'Whoops! I just grabbed them because they were on special offer to make you laugh. I didn't look too closely. I hope you don't expect me to take them back!'

'No, but as punishment you must come round and change the occasional nappy!'

'Eeeugh!' squeaked Helen, 'I thought my job was to take him or her on picnics and outings to the park for a go on the swings and whatnot, not change the nappies.'

'Well, now you know what Godmothers are for,' said Rosalind grinning broadly.

'God ... what? Really! You want me to be a Godmother?!'

'Certainly, unless you have joined some weird religious sect since we worked together.'

'Thank you!'

'Not at all. Actually Mike and I are not really religious so it is an honorary title really. One step up from Auntie, if you like.'

-oOo-

It was absolutely pouring and it took Martin a minute or two to find the correct setting for the windscreen wipers as he got into his car after work.

Martin had driven in rain before in two or three of his lessons, but not rain like this. It was teeming down, and Martin wondered if he shouldn't wait few minutes for it to calm down before he risked driving out of the car park.

But then as the wipers offered occasional views ahead, something astonishing caught his eye.
There, standing at the uncovered bus stop on the corner was Dawn DeSantos, and with no umbrella she was getting soaked.

Martin did not hesitate. He put the car into gear, stalled, restarted it, selected the correct gear and then carefully drove up to the bus stop, where he wound down the window a bit and called out.

'Hello, Dawn. Would you like a lift? Hop in!'

'Martin? You've got a car? Thank you!'

And Martin couldn't believe his luck when Dawn DeSantos got into the passenger seat of his car!
A very wet Dawn DeSantos admittedly, but there she was, in his car, in person.

'A good job I spotted you there,' he said, 'Have you ever seen rain like this!'

'Thank you very much, Martin,' said Dawn, looking at him speculatively from under a dripping fringe, 'I didn't know you had a car.'

'Oh yes,' said Martin, 'Well, I need it for work when I have to go and value houses and put them on the market, you see.'

'I see,' said Dawn, looking around and taking in the freshly vacuumed interior, 'Very nice. I didn't know you had passed your test.'

'Yes, although not long ago, to be honest. What do you think of the car?'

'It's a nice colour. It's a Polo, isn't it?'

'No, a Golf actually. Sort of the Polo's big brother.'

'Well it is very kind of you to offer me a lift, I was getting drenched!'

'So I saw. Are you going straight home?'

Well, well, thought Dawn. Martin must be doing really well. A Golf must be expensive to insure for someone his age. He was driving nice and carefully and not trying to show off too, so different from some his age.

'So are you enjoying working at Stiffhams?'

'Oh, yes, it's great, and I am getting more involved with the work the manager does now so they seem to appreciate me there. How is it going at the solicitors' office?'

Dawn threw caution to the wind. She could have bluffed it out with some nonsense about it being great, but this new car driving Martin seemed much more grown up now, and she had known him since the third year so she didn't really need to pretend to him.

'Well to tell the truth, just at the moment, it's awful.' She found she had a little catch in her voice and Martin glanced at her with concern as she decided to tell him the whole story.
She told him about Pauline Patrick, Leering Ledger, and Orlando.
'It horrible working there now and quite honestly I'm beginning to think I'd be better off working for my father at Antonio's restaurant!'

Having executed a rather slick left turn at the traffic lights, Martin expressed his surprise and sympathy and, as she blew her nose and hiccuped away a tear, he asked if she was all right.

'No, not really, and I'm not looking forward to going home to an empty house, to be honest. All my family are at work at the restaurant you see, getting ready for this evening, and I'm not involved in that any more.'

'Erm ...' said Martin uncertainly, 'Well, if you are not in a rush to get home, we are just coming up to Miriam's Tea Room, by the recreation ground, if you fancy a cup of coffee or something to warm you up while you dry out ...'

'Yes, Martin, that is a good idea. Lets do that.'

Blimey, thought Martin. I've just got a sort of date with Dawn DeSantos, no less. It's the old cupid magic again perhaps, unless of course she is just impressed with the car!

-oOo-

Geoff was pleased to be able to have a quiet evening on his own with Janet again, now that Bobbie had gone.

Janet was bottling up her feelings about her brother, if that was who he really was, and he wanted to help her to deal with that.

He prepared a Caesar salad with homemade dressing for them both. He had only a very limited culinary range, having rarely been allowed to use the kitchen by his wife because she said he always made too much mess and never put things back where they belonged, but he could knock up a pretty tasty dressing and grill a bit of chicken to go in the salad; although he had cheated by buying ready-made croutons.

As he poured Janet a glass of wine and handed it to her, he broached the subject that was obviously troubling her and out it all came.

'I can't believe I was so foolish,' she said, 'It would appear that he was a con man, just wanting me to pay for his nursing care. I feel so stupid.'

'He can't have known all those years ago that he was going to end up needing nursing care,' Geoff offered, 'It might have been *you* that needed to draw money from the Trust fund, you know.'

'I suppose so. But I paid in so much money and he might not even have been my brother.'

'But I thought you said that the joint life insurance policy would pay all that back when the Probate comes through.'

'They actually said it would pay back most of it, and I bet once the lawyers have extracted their pound of flesh, it will reduce considerably.'

'Well, we don't know that yet. We will just have to wait and see. What are your feelings about his wife?'

'That is strange, isn't it,' said Janet taking a deep draught of her wine, 'Why do you suppose he kept quiet about her? I mean we weren't exactly close in recent years, but that is a pretty big thing to keep from your sister.'

'Well, do you think if he told her about you it might mean he had to reveal stuff about his past he didn't want her to know?'

'Oh I don't know, Geoff. It all very confusing and quite honestly, given what that detective said, we might never get to the bottom of it. I suppose it is lucky that there was that insurance policy to mop up some of the financial damage, but on an emotional level Barry seems to have done no end of harm.'

Janet reached for a tissue to wipe her eyes as Geoff moved to squeeze her hand.

'I think he was just looking for love,' he said, 'Maybe he did it in controversial ways, but I didn't really understand the power of love until I met you, and I can see how someone might be driven by it.'

'Oh, Geoff!' said Janet, standing up and knocking her almost empty wine glass over as she fell into his arms.

-oOo-

'What? Nothing at all?' Sylvia asked.

'No, the idea is you bring your own furniture and so on to help you feel quickly at home. We will provide just an empty room. You can decorate it as you like, of course, but it will need carpets and curtains as well as furniture.' Margaret paused for breath, 'And I did explain that we have three rooms available but only one is en-suite, and a little more expensive, didn't I?'

Thank goodness the young couple had turned down her offer of all her furniture, she thought.

'Perhaps I had better come down again and have a look at the actual rooms this time,' she said.

'That's fine and it will be nice to see you, only ...'

'Only what?'

'Well, the guest room is booked up solid for the next two months, you see. You could always bring a tent if you have one,' Margaret offered. 'There is plenty of space in the garden.'

-oOo-

With the police report submitted and no further action required, the Senior Partner was able to complete the Probate application.

He was a little surprised to see that Pauline had made an appointment to see him and realised that he would also have to tell her that Dawn, her trainee, had decided to leave and go to work for her father. With no secretary in the department and that Spanish chap about to go back to college, the Conveyancing Department was looking very precarious.

After the initial preliminaries, Pauline asked how long the Probate might take now and explained that she was thinking of taking a holiday.

On receiving his answer to that, and on learning that Dawn had resigned, she seemed to be groping in her bag for something.

'Well,' she said now, drawing out a white envelope, 'I'm afraid I also have some news for you. This is my resignation.'

The Senior Partner was quite taken aback and for a moment struggled for words.

'What? Why? What?' he blustered, so Pauline repeated her statement and said that she wanted to leave straight away without returning to work.

'But that means we will have no staff in Conveyancing. Who is going to deal with the outstanding cases?'

'Perhaps you could, or maybe you could ask Mr Shotter if he wants his job back on a part-time basis … When he returns form holiday of course,' Pauline smiled.

'Er, Mr Shotter is on holiday, you say?'

'Not yet, but he will be next week. You see he and I are going to Ballybunion in Ireland. We are going to stay in my hotel there to see what it is like. Separate rooms of course, and we shall have to go as paying guests as the Probate is not through yet, but I can certainly afford to treat him to thank him for all his recent kindness, or at least I will be able to shortly. And after that I shall retire.'

She left the Senior Partner sitting ashen-faced at his

desk with his mouth open. The day had not turned out as he had expected at all.

-oOo-

EPILOGUE

Dawn had enjoyed her first few weeks working 'front of house' with Stefano. Her father could barely contain his delight at her joining the family business at last and had been generous with the salary he offered her.

Tonight however, Dawn had the evening off. She had just finished filing her nails and she surprised herself at how good they looked. Much shorter now, of course, as was appropriate for working in a catering business, even if she wasn't actually cooking, but still stylish and healthy looking.

A sort of strangled 'toot' outside, which sounded more like a sheep bleating than a car horn, told her that Martin was outside. Tonight they were going to the cinema.

-oOo-

Rosalind struggled to her feet.

At least there wasn't long to go now, but she was too hot and getting down on the floor to paint the skirting boards was becoming hard work.

At least the stark lounge and their bedroom was done now, and she had told Helen she was very pleased with them, although she said so herself.

They had decided not to paint the baby's room yet until they knew if it was a boy or a girl. They could have found out, but had decided not to. Not knowing was part of the excitement; and to start with, there would be a cot in their bedroom, of course, so there was no rush.

The rest of the house, which seemed ever so big compared to their little flat, could wait, and as everything was just painted white, when they bought it, it was not too bad, so would do for now.

She had better start getting ready. Mike would be home soon and then he was taking her to Helen's hen party.

She smiled when she thought about that and how her friend had arranged things so that there was barely two weeks between the hen party and the wedding itself. Having finally got her wish and got Paul to set a date, Helen was not going to leave anything to chance and wanted it over and done as quickly as possible.

Mike was going to the stag do tomorrow, of course. But he was getting a taxi.

-oOo-

Sylvia had been a bit extravagant with the carpet and the rug she chose, but she was pleased with her choice now.

She had never tried yoga before, but Margaret was pretty experienced at it and as they twisted themselves into ever more unlikely knots in her room, she was glad to have a nice soft floor covering beneath her.

She had had to sell or give away a lot of stuff to charity, of course, as there was no way it would fit in her room at the retreat, but with its big sunny bay window and French doors to the garden and cosy en-suite shower, she was very happy with it.

Bryn was happy too, or at least she supposed he was. He had even sent her a hand-made 'Good Luck In Your New Home' card before she moved. He didn't think to write his new address on it though, so she could not send him one back, but that was typical.

-oOo-

The house had sold surprisingly quickly. Just four viewings and an offer of the asking price.

Geoff had been delighted to tell Janet that he could honour his side of the deal and pay for half the house when they found one, and although she said he didn't have to, especially as Barry's insurance policy would now pay out, it did his pride good to know that he could.

Meanwhile Janet had reduced the price of 2 Easton Drive and received an offer almost immediately. That meant she was climbing into the Jaguar now, as Geoff held the door for her, clutching armfuls of estate agent's details. They had an appointment tomorrow to meet somebody called Martin from one of the agents at the first house on their list, but they wanted to look at the outside and the area again first to make sure about it.

Then they were meeting Lucy at the local pub just round the corner for a drink.

-oOo-

The manager of the Dublin Social Services department and the owner of the nursing home where Miss Siobhan O'Toole lived got their heads together.

They had been trying to contact Mr Patrick for months but only had his London address, and it seemed he had moved away. Now they had heard from the police and then this English solicitor about his death.

They were able to tell the police, who agreed to tell the English solicitor fellow, that Siobhan's long lost illegitimate daughter had turned up months ago with all sorts of proof as to who she was, and whilst it was very kind of Mr Patrick to keep sending them £1,000 a month towards her care costs, he didn't need to do it now because the daughter could prove that he was not related to her and that *she* was; and anyway, hadn't social services said they would pay for her care now? They didn't need Mr Patrick's money and would he be wanting some of it back?

The Senior Partner, acting in his role for the Estate of Mr Barry Patrick, contacted the bank and stopped the standing order straight away and sent the nursing home and the Social Services people a confirmatory note with his thanks.

-oOo-

Bobbie was staying at 2 Easton Drive again for the weekend.

Somehow or other she had managed to wangle herself an interview for a job with Oakshott, Parslow and Partners, who as it happened were the same solicitors acting for Geoff in the matter of his divorce.

The job was in the Conveyancing Department and when she got there, apparently she met this gorgeous Spanish chap who was in the process of handing over the work to some old boy who looked about a hundred and ten years old.

Bobbie didn't fancy working in what she described as a scene out of Dickens, and not a very good one at that, but she had been asked on a date by the gorgeous Spanish chap.

'So when you see a Porsche draw up outside, Uncle

Geoff, that will be for me. I may still be slapping on the makeup when he arrives as one likes to look one's best.'

And a little later the car did pull up and the Spanish chap rang the doorbell.

'Hola, Bobbie,' he said, 'I a hope is OK, I have a booked a table at a restaurant called Antonio's. I not been there myself but the people in the office, they say is best one round here. You look very nice. You ready? We go?' and they went.

-oOo-

Ballybunion in County Kerry, Ireland had woven its spell on Pauline in no uncertain terms.

Now, about to leave for her third visit there she had decided to make it her permeant home and was going to look for a house to buy. But first she had an appointment to keep at her own house.

She was expecting a Mr Martin Dartnell-Parkes, from Stiffhams Estate Agents to turn up to measure up the house and put it on the market.

Now that she had access to Barry's money, she was going to enjoy herself, and there was nothing to keep her here, after all.

-oOo-

Ivor 'Tiny' Washington watched the computer screen as he checked his bank balance once again.

This time he smiled broadly when the figures appeared. The payment had come through at last.

He began to dream of that trip to Florida again and, closing his laptop gently, he reached for the telephone.

Since it had been established that Stokes and Potts solicitors had ceased trading some years ago, there was nobody to threaten to lodge an action for the theft of a handful of sheets of headed notepaper and although there was still a question as to whether Barry Patrick really was Janet Bassett's sister, that did not affect the life insurance payout Tiny had just received.

Years ago, when Barry suggested that he and Tiny could insure each others lives, he had been silly enough to imagine that it was because Barry had some feelings for him.
He knew he loved Barry and, at that stage in their relationship he had hopes that perhaps one day Barry would return his affection. That was not to be, of course, but under those illusions he had taken out a not insubstantial joint life insurance policy on both of their lives and continued to pay the premiums ever since.

He now saw that all Barry wanted was the commission on the sale of the policy, but since he died there was no question that this little bit of Barry's greed and Tiny's gullibility had paid off.

As of ten fifteen this morning, Tiny Washington was

what is known in insurance circles as moderately wealthy.

As he was packing up to leave the office, Clive put his head round the door.

'Presume you have heard,' he said, 'Old Barry Patrick has died. Everybody loved dear old Barry Patrick.'

Yes, they did, thought Tiny, and he hoped Barry knew it.

THE END.

Disclaimer:

Note: All rights reserved. No part of this book, ebook or manuscript or associated published or unpublished works may be copied, reproduced or transmitted by any means, electronic, mechanical, photocopying or otherwise, without the prior written permission of the author.
Copyright: Bob Able 2022

The author asserts the moral right under the Copyright, Design and Patents Act 1988 to be identified as the author of this work.

This is a work of fiction, Any similarities between any

persons, living or dead and the characters in this book is purely co-incidental.
The author accepts no claims in relation to this work.

Acknowledgements:

With grateful thanks to John LeSueur for the story of the junior estate agent and the pen, which he assures me actually happened to him in his first job, shortly after he left school.

My thanks also to Andy Crabb for all his help, guidance and painstaking proofreading.

Bob Able:

If you like Bob Able's distinctive writing style and would like to read more of his work, here is a little more information…..

About the author:

Bob Able is a writer of fiction, thrillers and memoirs who describes himself as a 'part-time expat' splitting his time between coastal East Anglia in England, and the Costa Blanca in Spain.
He writes with a lighthearted touch and does not use graphic descriptions of sex or violence in his books, that is not his style. He prefers to leave that sort of thing to the reader's imagination.

'Spain Tomorrow', the first book in his popular and amusing memoir series was the **third most popular travel book on Amazon** in late 2020 and with its sequel, **'More Spain Tomorrow'** it continues to attract many good reviews and an appreciative audience in Europe, The United Kingdom, the USA and beyond.

His fictional novels include **'No Point Running'**, **'The Menace Of Blood'** (which is about inheritance, not gore) and the sequel **'No Legacy of Blood'** and are fast-paced engaging thrillers, with a touch of romance and still with that signature gentle Bob Able humour.

His semi-fictional memoir **'Silke The Cat, My Story'**, written with his friend and wine merchant, Graham Austin and Silke the Cat herself, is completely different. Cat lovers adore it and so do readers across the generations. Silke is a real cat, she lives today in the Costa Blanca, and her adventures which she recounts in this amusing book really happened. **Now available as an audio book** so you can listen to Silke telling you her adventures herself!
All Bob's books are available from Amazon as paperbacks or ebooks.

What's next? Well, there is another new series coming featuring **Bobbie Bassington** who we first met in Double Life Insurance. The first book **'Bobbie and the Spanish Chap'** is out now and by the time you read this it should be joined by **'Bobbie and the Crime Fighting Auntie'** and **'Bobbie and the Wine Trouble'**. These are amusing stories with a twist, that would make great beach reads. They feature the trademark Bob Able lighthearted writing style and engaging 'unputdownable' plots.

You can send Bob an email at the address below, to request details of release dates. The email address below is live and will reach him in person.

You can find details of how to buy all Bob's books, ebooks and even an **audio book** of '**Silke The Cat, My Story**' and follow him at:
www.amazon.com/author/bobable
Or just enter **Bob Able books** on the Amazon site and the full list should appear. For Audio books check out **ACX.com**

Or contact him directly at:
bobable693@gmail.com

Thank you for reading. You may like to know that Bob regularly contributes a proportion of the royalties from his books to 'The Big C', Norfolk's cancer charity, who have helped Bob with his own cancer battle and who do great practical work to help cancer victims and promote research.

Find out more at:-
www.big-c.co.uk

Incidentally, Bob is looking for a new Publisher and a 'literary Agent' to represent him ... any ideas?

Printed in Great Britain
by Amazon